# The Secret Diary of an

# ARRANGED MARRIAGE

## HALIMA KHATUN

A HAYAT HOUSE book
First published in Great Britain in 2020 by Hayat House.
Copyright © Hayat House 2020
The moral right of Halima Khatun to be identified as the author of this work has been asserted by her in accordance with the Copyright, Design and Patents Act, 1988.
Cover design by Felix Diaz de Escauriaza
All the characters in this book are fictitious, and any resemblance to actual persons living or dead is purely coincidental.
Paperback ISBN: 978-1-9163183-0-4
A CIP Catalogue record for this book is available from the British Library

To my mother, a trailblazer in her own right and my husband, who never stopped believing in me, even when I doubted myself.

# Just for you... Because there's two sides to every story

This story is all about our heroine. It's her journey, her struggles, her learnings. But of course, for every story, there's another side. When you get to the end, you'll get the opportunity to hear from the boys – the heroes, anti-heroes, false heroes... whatever you'd like to call them. But for now, enjoy getting to know our heroine. You'll like her, she's quite funny.

# 7th March, I'm getting married

I'm getting married and you're invited. I can't share too much yet, mainly because I don't know where, when or who I'll be marrying. But that's just a minor detail. The main thing is, by hook or by crook... it's happening.

One may wonder... without a venue, save the date, or indeed a man, how can I be so sure? Well, I'm 25, I've finished my degree (and masters, I'll have you know) and I'm having a good pop at this working lark, with a promotion on the horizon at my PR company. With education done and work bubbling along nicely, it's time to think about something bigger. In fact, the biggest step of my life - finding a man and getting married.

Most girls think about settling down at some point (unless you're a modernist, feminist sort). But for me, marriage comes with a slightly greater sense of urgency than most. I'm Asian, you see. Bengali, if you need specifics. Being Bengali, finding a suitable suitor needs to come sooner rather than later, by whatever means possible.

Welcome to the world of the arranged marriage.

This is where we are matched up to an appropriate candidate based on education, occupation, family background and village 'back home'. Despite sounding terribly old-fashioned, arranged marriages have come a long way since generations gone by. Nowadays, we're allowed to get to know *and* like our prospective husbands. We even have a say in the small matter of the man we choose. How thoroughly progressive.

As I embark on this journey, I thought it best to write my thoughts for posterity. I'd like to turn this diary into a blog one day (anonymous, of course). Or if I don't find 'the one', I might burn it in an angry rage. Either way, I want to remember this time. The good, the bad and the ugly (and I don't mean just the boys). Plus, writing is not only the foundation of my career, it is my therapy, my solace and route to rational thinking. I'm hoping I'll come out the other side (hopefully) married, wiser and able to help the rest of womankind navigate the choppy waters of single-but-looking life.

Another reason for writing (and maybe sharing) this is to tell my side of the story. The story nobody hears. The story I've been complicit in burying through years of denial. I know many people have a bad opinion of arranged marriages. Living in a white area, I grew up listening to negative opinions on the subject from people who don't really know anything about it. To survive and fit in, I inadvertently fed the narrative by whitewashing what is a fundamental cornerstone of my culture. I simply don't talk about it to my friends, because apart from one very worldly girlfriend whom I adore, most would be shocked that I'd even entertain the idea of being set up by my family.

Work colleagues are equally oblivious to my impending manhunt. If they knew, I imagine they'd worry that I'm being forced into a backward, sexist tradition that has no place on British soil.

I don't blame people for thinking the worst. Every single book, TV show or movie that depicts arranged marriages paints a sad picture. At best, it's seen as a last resort for desperate singletons. At worst, it's a breach of basic human rights. And it always, always goes against the wishes of the girl.

So with the safety of anonymity, I'd like to do something I've never done before. I'd like to talk about it, starting with some myth-busting.

First, you're not forced into marrying any old Joe (or more likely, Junaid) chosen by your parents. That's called a forced marriage, hence *force* is applied. Nor are you made to marry someone you meet for the first time. The 21st Century arranged marriage affords you several meetings, some official (i.e. mum and dad know about it), many unofficial (though your mum probably knows about it) and a frequent exchange of text messages to boot.

There's none of this get-married-to-the-first-boy-that-comes-along nonsense either. Most girls I know have met several prospective suitors before getting married. My sisters met quite a few, while my cousin Rashda – who's a brown Angelina Jolie lookalike - went into double figures. Such was her revolving door of men (in a non-slaggy way) that she started getting their names and occupations mixed up (again, in a non-slaggy way).

Yes, the mechanics of an arranged marriage are a bit formal but it's not quite as bad as non-Asians are led to believe. And here's the real revelation - the bit you *never* get to hear about... many of us Bengali girls are open to being set up in this way. Shocking, I know.

Now I've established what it isn't, here's what an arranged marriage actually *is*...

An arranged marriage is basically the precursor to Tinder and Match.com. While Match.com thinks it's a market leader with its complex algorithm helping determine who is the right partner for you, us Asians have been doing this since time began. We've long had someone else decide who is right for us. We didn't even need a computer.

It starts with our parents, who put the word out that they are 'looking for someone' for their son or daughter. They ask their extended family, though said family rarely like to recommend someone, as they too are looking to get their daughter married and don't want to be pipped to the matrimonial post. Or, these competitive aunties may offer their cast-offs - boys that are too fat, too short, too ugly or too uneducated for their darling child.

After exhausting that option, parents then cast their net wider. Luckily there are many busybodies in the community, who are more than happy to fix us up with some random whom they know nothing about but have heard they're from a 'good family'.

Nowadays, there are even professional busybodies. They play matchmaker as a side gig, charging willing (read: desperate) families a small fee for their efforts. These busybodies are usually middle-aged, bespectacled men who have an admin job in an all-Bengali office. Yet they somehow find the time to cultivate an excel spreadsheet with the names of people who are on the shelf, waiting to be plucked from single obscurity. They usually advertise their services in the local Bengali newspaper. They have a website that is always under construction and an email address that never works. Snail mail and telephone are their preferred modes of contact. I shouldn't really take the piss out of them though. The professional busybody enables us girls to meet more prospective boys than our mums ever did, in a short space of time, too.

Simultaneously, us youngsters do our own hunting. We go to thinly veiled marriage events, which are usually marketed under the guise of charity fundraisers. So much has been raised for Gaza by us singletons alone, we're likely to be the largest donors.

The more brazen of us go the whole hog, attending racially discriminate padlock and key events. My uni friend Reena, who is Hindu Gujarati (read: *way* more modern than us Muslim Bengalis) has attended a few of these events. She's not impressed, as she's found herself forced into conversation with other singletons that she doesn't remotely fancy as they may hold the key to her padlock. Apparently it's kind of like a business-networking event but with more pretentious twats.

The last resort, of course, is the Internet. Shoes, car insurance, courgette recipes and now husbands. Is there anything you can't find online?

There is one small issue, however. I'm caught in the middle. I've never fully fit in with my friends, colleagues *or* even my family. Big sis says I'm too westernised, as I don't like fish curry (it's the smell that gets me, and I don't like fiddly bones). My friends have likely cottoned on that I'm absent from every booze-fuelled night out but turn up with a spring in my step for lunch dates. While my work colleagues have noted that I duck out of socials at 11pm, just as Peter gets drunk and 'handsy'. How nobody has raised this with HR yet is beyond me (Peter's misconduct that is, not my unsociable ways).

I know *I'm* a misfit, but I don't know if there is anyone like me of the single and male variety. From what I've seen, most other Bengalis are either very cultured or not cultured at all. So there'll likely be some element of compromise. But at this stage, with my somewhat limited life (and boy) experience, I'm not sure what's got to give.

So there's the challenge...

I don't want to be single forever. I want to stop sharing a bedroom with my teenage sister. I want the big Bengali wedding with the sparkly lehenga. I want to have kids at some point.

But in terms of who I wear the lehenga for and who I have kids with, is a harder one to call. Beyond knowing that I want to get married, I don't really know what – or who - I'm looking for.

# 28<sup>th</sup> March, The pity

Living in a small town outside Manchester and working in a PR company on the outskirts of the city, I have always found myself to be the only brownie in the village (and office). Therefore, I am inadvertently the spokesperson for arranged marriages and I am quizzed on the subject in the most random, unexpected and brazen of ways.

Just last week I was having a conversation at work with Peter, who is every inch the serious PR Director when he's not had two glasses of Prosecco, about the upcoming Christmas lunch. We were lamenting the lack of food options when Fiona, who'd just returned from the kitchen with her third cup of black coffee that morning, piped up and asked: "So will you have to have an arranged marriage?"

You couldn't make it up. I mean, where the *hell* did that come from? It's not like we were talking about cultural norms in Bangladeshi society. How did we go from garlic mushrooms to arranged marriages? There wasn't even a smooth transition. In fact, there wasn't even a transition. Even the smallest of segues would have helped.

Clearly, Fiona had it on her mind and felt she just *had* to ask. It was like a knee-jerk reaction. A spontaneous burst of invasive nosey-ness. She couldn't wait until a relevant subject came up. Nor could she afford me the good will of waiting until we were alone. She had to shout it across our open-plan office.

The makeshift walls separating each desk offered no privacy, or in this case, dignity. Everyone heard.

I felt my face heat up. If I weren't so brown I'd be bright red at this point. My corner of the room fell deathly quiet. A few people looked up from their desks. Peter, whose ruddy cheeks were now brighter than his salmon pink shirt, seemed to do all the blushing for me. He stared at me with what looked like a combination of pity and genuine intrigue. Obviously this was far more interesting to him than my food choice for the Christmas party but he still felt sorry that I was singled out. Others looked like they were just relieved she asked, as it's something that had been bugging them ever since the brown girl joined the team. Which was two years ago, by the way.

I nervously took a sip of my tea, forgetting that it's piping hot. I nearly burned my tongue. I was embarrassed and mortified. A 'difference' had been identified so publicly and not the first time. All my life I've been reminded of my brown-ness with such blatant disregard to my feelings. Fiona's imposition sent me back in time, to my teenage self – awkward, reserved and trying to fit in...

In school, I remember Carly, the only mixed-race girl in our Year, wanting to know the names of each of my sisters. An innocent enough query, you may think. Except, like Fiona's unfiltered line of questioning, this came left of field and was shouted from the other end of the classroom. When I responded, she repeated each name, painfully slowly, struggling to pronounce each syllable. And honestly, their names aren't that difficult to say. I'd tell you what they are but that would blow my cover. More to the point, Carly couldn't give a toss about my sisters' names. She had an ulterior motive.

To fit in herself, conniving Carly was adopting a rudimentary tactic - pick on the other ethnic minority. You know, the one who's even browner. The one whose navy school jumper is a size too big. The one who's never allowed to get drunk in the park, go out with the boys, or any of the other stuff that she could do. It wasn't quite bullying, it was more of a sport.

The worst thing of all of this was the pity that came with it. The looks from other kids. The looks that said *sorry you're being picked on, sorry you're different*. I could almost, *almost* cope with being singled out, if nobody else would notice, or even care. But they noticed and they felt bad for me.

It was only Julia who defused the tension by saying: "I love your sisters' names. They beat ours – Julia and Jem-my-ma. They go with the matching outfits mum made us wear since the day we were tiny. Which wouldn't be so bad if we weren't FOUR YEARS apart!"

Julia always had my back and I laughed a little too heartily as a thank you. I think it was at that point that I learnt my best form of defence was humour.

These incidents peppered my school life. I was asked whether my parents could speak English (for the record, they can, in a very broken way). Another popular one was whether I had curry every day (and I did, except on oven-chips-Tuesday and the occasional fish-finger-Friday). It was only when I moved away for University and made some Asian friends, that suddenly my differences weren't so different. Yes, my friends had less strict and younger parents but the fundamentals were the same. At the very least, we all had funny foreign names.

Alas, university was a bubble. I graduated, came back home and now I work for a company in the sticks. Life has come full circle. Here I am once again – awkward, trying to fit in, and fielding stupid-ass questions from people who really have no business asking. Even the looks of pity, in adults instead of pre-teens, are the same.

I should be used to it by now but I'm not. Each time I'm ambushed feels like the first time. That stomach knot. That face flush. It doesn't get any easier. For my sins, I responded how I always would – with denial. My parents can speak the Queen's English. I don't eat curry every day. And I most certainly won't have an arranged marriage.

Fiona was visibly relieved by my response, which she then followed up with an anecdote of her own. "There was an Indian girl that I used to work with at my old company and she had a boyfriend but she couldn't tell her family. She said they'd hit the roof if they found out, as they wanted her to have an arranged marriage. I remember feeling really sorry for her."

This then prompted other eavesdropping colleagues to chime in with their two pence worth of "oh, that's awful" and "how unfair."

And it is awful. But like everything else I've seen on TV and read about in books and newspapers, this only shows one side of a whole unknown world.

'Love marriages' have been quite the norm for years and I'm planning on doing my own hunting. But arranged marriages *do* still very much exist. And I'm going into the process with open eyes and an open mind. However, I wasn't about to let nosey cow Fiona know that, nor anybody else, for fear of highlighting what most people see as a problem with Asian society. Though I'm about to poke holes in this viewpoint. Arranged marriages are NOT A PROBLEM.

For too long there's been a misunderstanding but arranged marriages are actually a bloody brilliant idea. They're a dead cert against being a spinster and growing old alone. It's a cast-iron guarantee that no matter how ugly, how fat or how boring you are, there will be someone for you.

In this modern western society we live in, how many people do you know who are in their thirties, or even forties, that are single? I bet you know someone. I do. Her name's Laura and she's my eldest sister's friend. She's in her late thirties, never quite got on the dating ladder and possibly never will. Having been single for so long, she doesn't have the confidence to meet someone new.

The BBC says there's a spread of loneliness in Britain, a growing epidemic of people living in isolation as they haven't settled down and are facing old age alone. This is where the arranged marriage would have come in handy. In western culture, you're left to it. If you're single, it's not really anyone's problem but your own. In Asian culture, it's *everyone's* business and mission to find you a match. The process may be daunting, cringe-worthy and borderline comical but you're pretty much guaranteed a suitor at the end. If you find someone of your own accord, even better. I'd like to. But if I don't, I can take comfort in the fact that I've got my arranged marriage trump card to fall back on.

I wish I had the balls to say all this to Fiona. But it's hard. We work together, speak the same language and drink tea from the same stained office mugs. We have more similarities than differences. But the arranged marriage is the one thing that the Fiona's of the world can't get their head round. To her, they're a strange brown phenomenon. It's an uncomfortable conversation to have in an open plan office, so if I do serialise this diary as a blog, I might just send Fiona a link.

Unfortunately, pity, confusion and misunderstanding isn't just confined to the office in my world. Even my best friend Julia sometimes struggles to get her head around it, even though she's possibly the brownest white person I've met.

I've known Julia since I was five and she's one of just a handful of friends I've kept in touch with from school. Not only did she come to my rescue when Carly played spot-the-other-brownie, she's never once asked an ignorant question, or put me on the spot. We made friendship bracelets for each other, gossiped about our high-school crushes (though she could pursue hers) and shared our ambitions in life.

Over the years, Julia's also had a few glimpses into my culture. She's seen my mum pick me up on my first day of school in a billowing floral saree. I was mortified. I mean, who picks up their kid from high school anyway? And don't get me started on the saree. She's been round for dinner. Though I think she was disappointed when it was fish fingers on the menu, rather than the chicken curry she could smell wafting in from the kitchen (mum thought it would help me better fit in by serving up an English meal. I had the chicken curry as a second dinner after Julia had left).

When Julia went and studied at a University full of Hindus, she became something of an expert in arranged marriages, courtesy of her more forthcoming brown friends. She even briefly dated an Indian guy who later had an arranged marriage with a girl from the community that he's known since he was six. So while Julia *kind of* understands the world of arranged marriages, she doesn't necessarily agree with it.

We meet for lunch at our favourite rustic Italian the weekend after the Fiona fiasco and I couldn't wait to tell her all about it. Partly because Julia loves hearing my work stories – she thinks PR is so glamorous compared to her role as a trainee family lawyer. But also, I wanted to know that I was right to feel offended and that Fiona was indeed a nosey cow.

Prim as ever, Julia arrives in what I would call smart business casual, with tailored trousers and a camel-coloured blazer. Her brunette hair is worn in her standard shoulder-length polka straight look. I'm half-wondering whether she's on call this weekend. I'm also wishing I'd made more effort. My hair hasn't seen a straightener since I washed it three days ago, so it's scraped back in a trusty ponytail. And I'm wearing Diesel jeans. I must have overlooked the dress-code.

Not only is she dressed for business, it seems that Julia can't shake off lawyer mode. She normally pipes up whenever she gets a whiff of ignorance but is surprisingly diplomatic about Fiona's intrusion. "The way she asked you could have been more... tactful but I think she was just intrigued. I suspect she doesn't get to interact with many Asian people, so the only thing she knows of your culture is what she sees on TV, which is hardly helpful."

No shit, Sherlock. In the last few years, according to the news, you'd be forgiven for thinking anyone Muslim is a terrorist, an oppressed woman, or both.

"But I didn't sign up to do the PR for all Muslims, so the idea that I'm a spokesperson available on tap for any personal questions is just a joke."

Seeing my offence, Julia holds her hands up. "You're right, she was out of order in the way she asked. But... like I say, people are just, well, interested."

Julia takes a long sip of her iced tea, downing with a visible gulp, as if she was preparing to deliver an uncomfortable home truth to a client. "And maybe she also wanted to check in on your... welfare."

"My welfare?" I see Julia's face change. I iron out the crease on the cotton red check tablecloth with my hand, pressing harder with each stroke. That crease has been annoying me since we sat down but the rough cotton material is strangely soothing, like it's scratching an itch.

Here comes the pity party.

Julia does her empathising (yet patronising) face, the one she reserves for divorcing couples going through mediation. "Look, I know about arranged marriages more than most... non-Asian people," she begins, avoiding eye contact and instead focusing on her unused knife, which she is running along the rim of her plate.

Julia and I are careful not to refer to each other as brown or white, though that is totally what we mean.

She continues, choosing her words carefully like the good lawyer that she is: "But I just... well, I worry about you sometimes. There. I said it. Oh, don't look at me like that." She smiles, trying to lighten the mood as she notices my grimace.

Julia rests her knife on the table. "I get that arranged marriages are the done thing. And God knows, sometimes I wish someone would sort me out with a guy. I've been single for two years now and it's getting boring. Plus, since I moved to London, dating is a nightmare. I thought it'd be easier to find someone decent there but nobody wants anything serious. But at least I'm getting to date..."

We suddenly realise that we have an audience, as the grey-haired couple next to us is making no secret of their eavesdropping. They're looking right at us, waiting for us to go on.

Julia lowers her tone. "And I'd love for you to date too. Let's be honest, you had your share of admirers in school, so if you got yourself out there – wherever 'there' is in Muslim culture, I doubt you'd be single for long. And even if you end up meeting someone through your family, I hope that you get to have the fairy-tale. You know, the date nights, the holidays... all those things."

Julia returns to her penne pasta, leaving me to ponder her point.

Her concerns aren't completely unfounded but her views are outdated. Growing up, it seemed that the wives of my cousins were of the brown Stepford variety. Whenever we'd visit, they'd be clad in a saree, serving samosas and being very polite and ladylike. Kind of the opposite of what I am. However, it's only in recent years that I realised that what we see on a very occasional visit is just a show. They're putting their best faces forward, making an effort for the guests. These seemingly desperate housewives were still having date nights, holidays and their very own fairy-tale. And how do I know all this? Facebook, of course, the giver away of all secrets.

Mum, who often reminds me that arranged marriages don't mean the end of a girl's life, confirmed my findings. "In fact, getting married can be the beginning of a lovely new phase, as you can travel and see the world with your husband and do things you no able do as single woman."

Times have moved on even further still. Girls nowadays ditch the saree-wearing formalities. They continue with their careers after marriage, earn their own money and are in charge of their own lives. They're not trapped in a lifeless, loveless marriage, as Julia believes.

Where Julia *is* right, however, is that with arranged marriages, we don't get too long to get to know somebody, so there's less time to know if they're the one. So what can seem like a fairy-tale at the beginning could well be just a dream. And does that concern me? Of course it does. Like any girl, whether she's Bengali, English or Mongolian, I want the fairy-tale. And just like any other girl, I worry that I might not get it. I worry that I won't find the one. That I'll have to settle. But I don't think this is just a Bengali issue, or even a brown one. I think this is something that keeps all single girls up at night.

The bill arrives and I know this is the last time I'll see Julia for a couple of months. I'm hoping that next time we meet, I'll have some positive news to share. Mainly because I'd love to meet someone and partly to show Julia that us brownies aren't as backward as she thinks.

"You know what, I hope we both get the fairy-tale. And for my part, I will do everything I can to find 'the one'. You'll be glad to know I won't be just relying on my parents."

Julia's pity face turns into a beaming smile. "And I can help you too on that front. I'm always meeting new people in Canary Wharf. So if I come across any nice Bengali boys, I'll let you know."

I'm highly doubtful that Julia will be a source of marriage-appropriate boys but I smile appreciatively.

# 1<sup>st</sup> April, Biodata

In order to have a queue of eligible men outside my door, mum tells me I need to get my biodata sorted. A biodata is like a marital CV. When you're looking for a job, you put together a CV, which highlights your occupation, education and hobbies. When you're looking for a spouse, you also put together a CV, which highlights your occupation, education and hobbies. You then add in your height and build and enclose a nice photo to boot.

I think a biodata is a lot more straightforward than a professional CV, as I don't need to list my key achievements or write a bullshit personal statement. Though I do need to write crap about myself to seem appealing enough to go past the first round and into the marriage interview, or rishtaa meeting.

I don't really know where to start. So, as I do with most things, I consult Google. A quick search of 'what to include in a biodata' throws up a list of threads, forums, guides and examples of how to market myself with my marital CV. Amazing.

The basics are:

- Name (obviously)
- Age (don't include D.O.B. though, as they'll know I'm nearly 26 and we can't have that)
- Hometown (not the full address. Want to keep stalkers at bay)
- Occupation

- Education (my degree isn't just useful for getting me a job)
- Height (this is very, very important)
- Parents' names (for the crucial research into the family)
- Name of the village in Bangladesh my parents come from (again, for research purposes)
- Parents' town address in Bangladesh (must include this to prove that we are middle-class and have a house in the town, not just a mud hut in the village)
- Siblings (to know how many Eid presents we must buy)

I throw all this info together in a word document and present it to mum, who's sat in our dining room, reading the Bengali newspaper she gets on a monthly subscription. It's handy that she's already wearing her glasses. She shifts her attention from the paper, clears her throat and sits up straight on the brown leather-backed wooden chair. She is taking this terribly seriously. While she reads, she makes lots of mum noises like '*hmm... ah... hmm*', before telling me my biodata isn't marketable enough.

She doesn't actually give me any constructive pointers but just shrugs her shoulders, saying in a mix of Bengali and broken English: "*Ammi zanni na*, it just doesn't seem interesting enough. I doh-no. Don't girls normally add a bit more detail? Maybe put in a line about what you're like as a person."

*What I'm like as a person?* Could she be any more vague? Plus, if I was to detail my true persona – very talkative, ambitious and lacking in girly grace, I'd probably have most prospective Bengali boys running for the hills.

Bemused and confused, I check out other examples. People sometimes include their build. I'm a size eight, with slightly wider hips. But I am loathed to describe myself as 'slim but pear-shaped'. If someone wants to know my build, they can deduce it from my photo, or see for themselves in person. They've got eyes.

This whole biodata compilation isn't as easy as I thought. I'm at a bit of a loss as to how to pimp my CV. It's also very annoying to learn that I do need to write a bullshit personal statement of sorts after all.

Adding to the pressure is mum, who is watching over me as I check out other biodatas online. She's taken to providing an unhelpful running commentary and getting totally distracted when she sees some photo examples of pretty girls clad in decadent Asian outfits. "Ooh, she looks *ni-iiice*, I bet *she'll* get snapped up quickly."

"Mum, that photo's from 1998, I'm sure she's married with kids now."

"Aww that's a shame. What about her? I wonder if she's still single? Does she look *Ban-gali* to you?" Mum points to a thumbnail of a girl in a green saree, posing with her arms around a tree trunk, like a Bollywood heroine.

"What the... why? You don't have any sons?"

"No, thank you for reminding. But I might know someone who knows a nice boy."

I think it's in every Bengali mum's genes to play matchmaker with someone, or anyone, so they can boast about their cupid credentials. However, with a very single daughter in her charge, mum really should remember her priorities.

As she doesn't have the displeasure of working at a computer 37.5 hours of the week, mum seems to find this whole ordeal fascinating and, dare I say, enjoyable. I, on the other hand, do not. And it's my biodata. So despite mum's eagerness to get it sorted - whilst getting sidetracked along the way – I ruin her fun by deciding to sleep on it. I have precious little patience for doing CVs at the best of times and this particular resume carries even more weight, as it's in preparation for the biggest job of my life.

With fresh eyes, I add a few bits to boost my biodata the next day. Without an audience, I can think more clearly. It helps that I'm editing in the almost privacy of my shared bedroom, rather than downstairs with mum being a backseat CV builder. I have to make do with little sis sat on her single bed, though luckily she's too busy playing with her phone to care what I'm doing. She is never not on her bed, nor off her phone. I swear that grey crushed velvet blanket has her shaped etched into it. Anyway, I add in that I'm family orientated (always a winner), though I'd assume this should be a given. I'd like to see a biodata where someone states that they hate their family and despise other people's kids.

Mum approves this second draft but warns me that my biodata must be tweaked depending on the prospective guy. I am *nothing* if not adaptable. Mum shares the biodata with dad but this is more out of obligation than anything else. She doesn't really want an opinion and she doesn't get one.

Dad spends less than 10 seconds looking at the fruits of my extensive Googling, barely reading the contents, before saying to mum: "Yes, yes, yes, it all looks fine to me. If you're happy with it, so am I."

After much editing, sub-editing and proofreading, both parents sign off my biodata. So next up is the bigger challenge, getting that all-important photo.

# 5<sup>th</sup> April, Pictures in the park

Well, that was bloody embarrassing.

When it comes to choosing an appropriate photo to send with the marital CV, most girls have a plethora of pictures to choose from. The fail-safe is usually a photo taken at someone else's wedding, where they crop themselves out of a group shot as they don't want to enclose a snap with the competition. A wedding is a great setting for a biodata photo because you're already decked out in your finery, your hair is coiffed and you've applied your makeup like an artist. You're ripe for the picking.

As mum and I scroll through the photo archives of previous weddings, it's another painful reminder that I am not most girls. We stare in silence at the snaps of me from the past two years. I know it, she knows it, but neither of us wants to say it out loud.

When I go to a wedding, something is always amiss. More often than not, my hair has let me down. I have naturally straight hair, which many girls would die for. Yet I try to curl it, with little success as the ringlets fall out within an hour. Or, I have practiced my bun/back combing/waves the night before and it worked a treat. However, such is the cruelness of life that on the all-important day itself, my hair would go pear-shaped. I'd suffer from a bout of unexpected greasiness, limpness, or anything else that would sabotage my hopes of a good hair day.

If you think that's bad, my hair is no competition for my makeup in the nasty stakes. My downfall is this: I have makeup thoughts above my station. I want to do a smoky-eye, or a highlight and contour. But the image I see on the YouTube tutorial I religiously follow, doesn't quite translate onto my face. I end up a smudgy, shiny mess. And these bastard photos have immortalised my aesthetic crimes.

"What about this one?" Mum points to a photo of me in a burnt orange saree. The saree looks good but there's a big foundation faux pas - my face looks suspiciously whiter than my neck.

"Hmm... maybe this one's better, I'm smiling at least," I say, clutching at straws.

She shakes her head. "Na na na... we can't use that one. You look *too* smiley. And your selva-kameez is much too tight. You need to at least try to look a lit-ool bit demure."

Only my mum could think smiling too much is a flaw. And for the record, that salwar kameez wasn't that tight at all. She really ought to see some of the spray on outfits my uni friends wore to the graduation ball.

Then mum has a lightbulb moment. "What about Salma's wedding last year, do you have pictures from there? You looked nice that day. That chocolate saree was beautiful and really pop your eyes."

Feeling like we might have uncovered a rare pearl, mum and I scroll through the photos to find that there are many pictures from Salma's wedding, just none of me. My sisters look great though.

It turns out that on the rare occasion I'm at a wedding and I look passably pretty, no bugger is at hand to take my photo. With other people's weddings out of the question, mum orchestrates a photo-shoot specifically for my biodata. I wear a nice but not-too-OTT pink salwar kameez and my makeup looks pretty good, if I say so myself.

After going on a recce around the house to find a suitable location, mum decides that our garden could provide a nice backdrop. Great in theory, even though our garden is less flowers and more tomato plants, raspberry bush and cabbage patch. But at least the outdoors will provide plenty of natural lighting.

However, theory doesn't always translate into practice. Getting my diminutive, adorable but very pushy mum to take a photo is a nightmare. It's hard to find your inner Kate Moss when your mum is shouting: "Smile... na that's too much... a smaller smile... just lit-ool, less teeth... put chin down."

Soon my false smile turns into a scowl.

Worse still, there's an audience. My little sister is pissing herself laughing as she watches from the upstairs window. Dad is skulking around in the dining room, pretending to read the Bengali newspaper, while twitching the net curtains and surreptitiously surveying the situation in the garden. I think he feels like it's not a dad's place to get involved. But as a father of four girls, he's seen his share of biodata photo-shoots and I bet he'd just love to get involved as a creative director.

Mum senses my discomfort. *"Horo in thaki!"* She waves her arm in an angry, hurried sweeping motion, just in case dad can't lipread through the window.

He retreats but then appears in the garden minutes later with a watering can. What in the actual *hell* is going on? Dad never tends to the plants and now is not the time to start. The last thing I need is a small, pot-bellied man sporting a sky blue panjabi and henna-tinted beard photo-bombing my snaps. His bright, summery look and jolly rounded features only serves to make me look even more moody.

"Why you here *now*? You can see we're busy!" Mum's patience with dad is wearing thin.

"I see, I see. But plants look dry, we have no rain for two days."

Mum scoffs at dad's excuse to join us in the garden. "We live in Manchester. If it not rained for two days, a flood will be on its way!"

I look up. Shitty sis is still laughing. I think she might even be taking her own behind-the-scenes snaps. How we will get a biodata-appropriate photo, I'll never know.

We examine the photos over tea. Our efforts are pitiful. Despite over 25 shots, none are really fit to share with other people, let alone potential suitors. My mum's turn as Rankin, combined with the unwanted attention, didn't help my pose. Also, the tomato plants failed to provide a scenic backdrop and the tan-coloured fence needs a lick of paint, as the photos revealed. So it turns out that the camera really doesn't lie. I bloody wish it would sometimes.

We decide to find another location. And where is the next best thing for sunlight and scenery? Why, the local park, of course!

After fending off dad, who wanted to join us under the guise of needing some fresh air, off we drive to our nearest park for some pretty outdoor-sy shots.

One thing that I didn't realise during the photo-shoot in the garden, is now *very* clear after a mid-shoot de-brief in the park. Mum is seriously cack-handed with a camera. I can't blame her as she is of a different generation but even so. She's cutting off my head, leaving a load of empty space on the left while I'm squished to the right... her photos are terrible.

"Mum, you can't even see my face in half these photos! What's the point in you taking charge when you don't know how to operate the bloody camera!"

"Ok, don't get *goosha with me*. Angry face makes you look miserable. These were just for practicing. Let's do more."

"You've done about 30 photos so far. How much more practice do you need? I knew I should have asked someone else to do this."

"Oh-ho! Who else take pictures? Your Julia? Hmmm, she'll have you in mini-skirt with legs out, then nobody marry you."

In all my years of knowing Julia, I have never seen her in a miniskirt. She's more of a below the knee kind of girl.

I can't just blame mum's shaky camerawork. The scenic park has presented an un-forecast problem, sudden winds. The strong gusts are blowing my scarf and billowing through my salwar bottoms, making me look like the genie from Aladdin. This is neither chic nor the desired effect.

The whole thing is embarrassing. While I have escaped my prying family, I've become the park's main attraction for dog-walkers. This is not helping as I'm shit-scared of dogs. A middle-aged woman, clad in a much more sensible thin raincoat, jeans and converse trainers, is pulled over in our direction by her hungry-looking bulldog. I feel my face heat up in sheer fear. This is not helping my foundation at all.

"Ooh you look lovely dah-ling," she says, struggling to pull on the lead as the muscle-bound canine comes closer, within biting distance.

"Aww, thank you," mum takes the compliment for herself. She adjusts the collar of her spring-inappropriate, fur trimmed camel-coloured coat.

Feeling obliged, the lady then turns to mum. "Oh and your saree is beautiful. I do love a floral print."

As her aggressive-looking dog pulls her away, mum nudges me. "See, English people love our clothes. I doh-no why you hate it so much."

"I don't hate it mum, I'd just rather not wear a salwar kameez in the park."

We have another audience. This time two old ladies head our way with scrappy little puppies. One runs towards me and sniffs around my ankles (the dog, not the old lady). I try to act cool, as I know my phobia offends dog lovers but I'm panicking inside.

The owner apologises, before telling me how lovely my outfit is. I don't know if she's being genuine or not. If nothing else, she probably thinks I'm a bit done up for the park. However, if she's seen *Bhaji on the Beach*, she might just think that's how my lot roll. On top of this, mum is providing comedy gold with her snap-happy ways. I'm mortified.

The weather is changing, switching between strong winds and unpredictable bouts of sunshine. Great - you may think. Sun is your friend. Well, it's not *my friend* when it's casting shadows all over the place, making me look darker than I am. Modern digital cameras may reduce red-eye but they can't do much about six o'clock shadows. And when you're already a brown Bengali, the last thing you want is to appear even more tan.

All of this is getting me rather stressed and interfering with my Zen. I am not in the zone, not feeling the good vibes and courtesy of my very open and honest face, I am not taking a good photo.

Mum, however, is a trooper. She is still insisting on taking more shots, getting me to pose, smile, lift my head, lower my head, smile again but not too much. However, her enthusiasm/ unintentional demotivation is not helping the situation. I'm turning tetchy. I'm also pretty sure my foundation has melted down my face. Clouds are forming. Bloody rainy Manchester. I give up in a huff and insist we go home. If the first 50 shots produced nothing of note, it's unlikely the next 50 will.

I may be flagging but mum isn't giving up. She WILL get me married and won't let a small thing like a bad photo get in the way. Seeing an opportunity when we get home, she takes some indoor shots, since I'm in my best get-up and all. By now the lighting's even worse as the sky has turned grey. It's about to chuck it down. We use the flash, hoping to capture *something* usable. However, the camera is cruel and highlights my shiny, angry face.

"Doorh! This house so plain *borrring*! We need some nice decoration. If I had son, he could paint walls brighter," mum moans.

"Well, it's your fault mum. You insisted on renter's magnolia when dad last painted. You can't expect him to redo it all only two years later. Especially with his bad back."

Mum ignores me. "Rashda's mum has beige walls with velvet design. It look posh and fancy. Very, very nice. Ok let's go near the flower picture."

Most people keep up with the Jones'. We're in a constant battle with the Mahmood's. I pose against the trio of pink flower canvasses, though they're much higher than my head. Then we try the overgrown aloe vera plant in the hallway as a backdrop. We test out some sitting on the sofa shots. It makes me look homely. Mum spends the next 30 minutes ferrying me from room to room, snapping at different angles and using the desk lamp as a studio light. Just WILLING me to take a good photo.

After a further ten or so shots, we call it a day. Examining the fruits of our efforts afterwards, there are a few OK ones, though nothing great. But after the day I've had, they'll have to do. I'm tired and I never want to see a digital camera again.

I have a question for mum. "How on earth did you manage to get good rishtaa photos of big sis back in the day? You couldn't see how the photos turned out until they were printed."

"Well, it was easier as she was -," mum pauses.

She was about to say prettier, fairer, more photogenic, or something along those lines but stops herself in the nick of time. I've heard such slights for as long as I can remember. Mum's said it, my siblings have said it. Outsiders have said it. It's always followed by an awkward pause and a sense of regret from whoever uttered it. I feel that familiar pang of pain and shame. Pain for being reminded that I'm not as attractive as my older sister according to the eyes of the Bengali community. Shame as though it's my fault. After years of practice, I thought

I managed to thinly veil my hurt but mum sees right through it. She's got years of experience too and rescues the situation in her usual way.

Mum stretches out her bottom lip in a grimace, something she does when she's worried about offending, or straight up lying. "I doh-no, we just got lucky," is her thought-through reply, saving both our blushes. The pain recedes in the familiar way.

Mum takes another look at the photos we've captured. She looks deflated and defeated. I'm sure she can't understand why other people's daughters take such nice pictures...

HAVING GONE THROUGH this ordeal today, I'd like to impart some advice. Girls, unless your mum is a professional photographer, please don't let her take your photo. Despite her best intentions, odds are she'll make a dog's dinner of it. Mums are too close to the project. They are perhaps the ones that want to see you happily married the most. So having them take your photo adds a whole lot more pressure to the situation. They're desperate for a good photo but their keenness will get in the way. Today I felt uncomfortable, under pressure and just harassed.

Do yourselves a favour. Get a girlfriend – who knows how to operate a camera - to take your photo. Have fun with it, relax and enjoy yourselves. If you're at ease, it'll show in the photos.

Failing that, pull your finger out and make a bloody effort when going to a wedding. Get up an hour earlier so you have time to do your hair. Do your makeup nicely and stick to what you know. Keep your look simple and you can't go wrong. Wear your best clothes and pose proudly on the main stage. And the most important lesson if you're taking a photo at a wedding is this – if you're in a group shot, stand next to the fat girl and crop out all those bitches that are prettier than you. Context is everything.

# 15<sup>th</sup> April, Thinly veiled marriage events

With my biodata now complete and photo ready (well, kind of ), I figured I ought to do my own hunting on the side to supplement my parents' matchmaking skills. I've decided to attend some Asian charity events. There's an abundance of them in Manchester. For me it's a win-win. For a cost of £20, I get a buffet dinner, raise money for Gaza/Pakistan/Lebanon *and* I increase my chances of bagging a husband. I'm helping others whilst helping myself. If that isn't value for money, I don't know what is.

I went to my first event last night. It was held at an impressively large banqueting hall in Cheetham Hill. The venue performs multiple functions. It provides a buffet by day, works as a wedding venue in the early evening and with this event, helps said weddings happen in the first place by bringing a bunch of single Muslims together at night.

The only downside is that Cheetham Hill is a nightmare to drive to for me, as it's on the other side of Manchester. I'm a nervous driver with no sense of direction at the best of times. As I was running late and driving to new territory, I made quite a few close calls. En route I got lost, went the wrong way down a one-way street and had to do a ten-point-park to squeeze my silver Ford Fiesta between two cars that were veering onto my bay. One car was a souped up BMW, no doubt owned by a pretentious twat who I hope I don't encounter at the event.

On arrival, I thought I'd got the wrong venue as I could only see families with young children sat eating. A kind waiter informed me that the event was taking place upstairs in one of their rooms for hire. I head upstairs to find that the room is decidedly less grand than the rest of the hall. It's a smaller, boardroom-style setup with dark mahogany furnishings. Tables are arranged lengthways to make a big square. The space in the middle houses a speaker and microphone, which I assume will be utilised by the event organiser. Unless there's a spot of karaoke on the itinerary.

Instead of risking life and limb to get here, I wish I'd taken my time. The event hasn't started and there seems to be some informal networking going on. Small groups of girls and guys are huddled in corners chatting, like there's some kind of invisible gender segregation. There's a real mixed bag of attendees. Some girls are wearing brightly coloured hijabs over black tunics, while others are sporting party dresses. There's not a salwar kameez in sight. I'm glad I opted for a black shift dress with a fuchsia pink shrug. The boys are more uniform, with most opting for dark suits, or spring-appropriate tan chinos. There's only one guy in jeans and even then, they're of the smart casual variety and paired with a blue work shirt. It's quite obvious that everybody has dressed to impress. Bloody charity, my arse.

I really wish I'd come with a friend. In fact, I wish I had Asian friends in Manchester, full stop. I could have used the safety in numbers. I don't think I can slip into one of these coquettish clusters, so I scan the room for other girls who are alone, vulnerable to an ambush. Luckily a petite woman arrives just after me, looking equally unsure of her surroundings. We get chatting. She's Pakistani and her name's Sophia. She's six years older than me and perhaps one of the few people there that's married and genuinely attending the event to raise money for charity. She's beautiful, so I'm not surprised that someone has snapped her up. She's also incredibly well put together, with her deep maroon silk dress and emerald green shawl – a perfect mix of East and West. I really wish I'd worn a shawl. I should have given more thought to my outfit, instead of reaching for the first dress that didn't need ironing. Sophia and I exchange numbers and will probably meet up again outside of a pretend charity event setting.

More excitingly, when Sophia excuses herself to answer a call from her husband, I stumble upon my next lonesome victim, a girl called Heena. Upon learning that I'm Bengali, she tells me she might know a suitable guy. She gets straight to the point as soon as we meet: "Are you looking?"

I want to reply: *Looking for what?* But I don't, as I totally know what she means. Plus I don't want to blow the potential opportunity of being set up on a date.

I act coy. "Um, not really."

"But you're not married, right?"

"No, I'm not."

"OK, so you're *kind of* open to looking?"

"I guess that's my default then." My nervous laugh kicks in.

Heena smiles knowingly. "Well, I *might* have someone for you."

Apparently this 'someone' is a pharmacist she knows through her work as a medical rep. A small part of me thinks this might be too good to be true. But a bigger, louder, more domineering aspect of my being is already thinking I'm onto a winner. I'm even kicking myself for not attending any of these events sooner. But of course, I act cool when she tells me about him, for fear of coming across desperate. I'm also mentally trying to work out how much a pharmacist earns per year. I suspect it's not quite up there with a doctor but still impressive nonetheless. She said she doesn't know him very well but she'll do some digging (via Facebook) to find out more.

Heena looks like she's in her late twenties and despite having the bodily proportions of Jessica Rabbit, she's still single. If *she's* still on the shelf, I'm not sure how much I fancy my own chances of finding a husband anytime soon.

Most people at this event are about her age, if not older. I'm actually one of the young ones here. This makes me wonder whether these pretend charity events are for those who've exhausted all other options. It also makes me realise that Asians are getting married later these days. Back in the day (I'm talking about ten years ago), 25 was pushing it. Now I'm practically a baby among old maids. I should bring my parents along to the next event to prove to them I'm not over the hill just yet.

"Salaam everybody, can I have your attention please?" A voice crackles on the microphone. "I'm Amjad and I'm your host for tonight. I do these events up and down the country. Most of you probably know me, though I think I see some new faces. If you're new to these events, please come and say hello to me, I don't bite... rrraff! Hm.... And, well... enjoy yourselves but keep things halal. Like the buffet – boo-boom!"

The microphone echoes, loudly and uncomfortably, like it's embarrassed for him. Amjad does a fake cough to drown out the tumbleweed silence.

"Umm... so sorry for the delay tonight, I was working late at my firm. My secretary was just about to give me another piece of work but I said '*Norma, charity waits for no man!*' Haha... So anyway, we've got a great night organised for you. And honestly, hand on heart; I take more pleasure in these events than I do any other aspect of my life. Mash Allah I've visited 27 countries, stayed in some of the best hotels in the world. But nothing satisfies me more than bringing great people together, for a great cause."

Amjad is a rotund, balding guy in his late-thirties who is likely to be single and probably here for the same reasons we all are. He's dressed to impress too, though his attire is more dad-at-a-party, layering a forest green half-jumper over a white shirt. His moment on the mic is milked for all its worth. He cracks some more bad jokes and plugs himself a little. Apparently, he's a well-travelled auditor (ladies, form an orderly queue). After delivering this self-promoting monologue, he introduces the icebreaker.

We each have a picture postcard at our place setting and we have to find the other person who has the same picture. I'm keeping my fingers crossed that my postcard will be matched up with a total fittie who just happens to be a doctor. Instead I get a really smiley hijabi girl called Mallika. Never mind. In truth, for all my bolshiness, I wouldn't really have the balls to chat to a fit doctor, anyway. The thing with being a Bengali girl is that I'm always conscious of treading the fine line between being friendly and loose when in male company. And at this event, it looks like EVERYONE is judging. So if you throw your head back laughing at a guy's bad jokes, you're a floozy. If you do that amongst a group of guys, you're a massive slut and unfit for marriage.

Judging by the unspoken protocol of this event, it looks like you should just stick with your girlfriends, look coy and hope that a doctor spots you and makes relevant enquiries as to who you are. It's all very Jane Austen-like.

I also found the event slightly bitchy. As everyone there is hoping to find a partner, very few people actually want to be friendly. It's a bit of a hunting ground of sorts, with more predators than prey. I tried talking to two very done-up girls who barely reciprocated. However, as soon as a group of blokes came to talk to them, they were all smiles, flicking their hair and flinging their heads back in exaggerated giggles. Yep, definitely floozies.

In terms of conversation - apart from Sophia and Heena - that wasn't too lively either. It actually felt a little pretentious and I had no choice but to roll with it. I found myself discussing the politics of Gaza where I really had no business, I'm just not that well informed. I also had to stay away from being too political, too vocal or too ignorant. I had my PR hat on outside of work. I felt like I was being interviewed, putting on a show and generally not being myself. In fact, I was so disingenuous that I turned into a bullshitter at the event. When I was asked why I've attended, I lied and said it's to make friends and raise money for such a worthy cause.

While both are kind of true - I donate to the exact same causes annually – charity and friendship weren't my top priorities. However, it doesn't seem appropriate to say: "It's time I got married, so along with my parents looking for me, I'm also doing a spot of shopping myself. So if you know of anyone..."

Despite this collective colluding of coyness, I would bet good money that everyone at the event – bar Sophia - was there for the same reason as me. Yet none of us dare admit it. I never understand why. Why are we embarrassed about wanting to find a partner? Why do we cringe at the thought of asking someone if they know someone? After all, no matter what race or religion you are, if you're 25 and single, you might be open to meeting someone, right? But we must never, ever admit it.

I remember when I was 22 and had just finished my master's degree, when an unexpected biodata came my way. The boy was 26, from Luton and someone that my big brother-in-law knew. I was not ready to get married, as I was keen to make my way in the world of work. Plus the thought of moving so far away from my family to build a new family filled me with fear. I told mum this and she agreed that I was too young, it was too soon and he was geographically inappropriate. But no sooner had she made that 'thanks but no thanks' call to the boy's family, I had a bout of rear-view syndrome. Should I *at least* have met him? Was I too dismissive? At 22, I felt that the world was my oyster and as for all the men in it... well, they could wait. This was the first prospective suitor. There'd be plenty more, I told myself. And when the time is right, I'll be up for being introduced.

After that, there were no more unexpected biodatas. In fact there were no more biodatas full stop. My brother-in-law decided not to ask after me as I'd rejected the first guy. Nobody has referred a boy since.

Three years of man-famine later, I'm now proactively hunting, while my mum occupies the role of hunter-gatherer. I don't want to advertise my single status. I'm embarrassed to say *please set me up* but that's precisely what I'm doing, in not so many words. Heena saw right through me. I'm single and looking but I didn't want to admit it. She had to drag it out of me.

This sense of embarrassment seems even more apparent for women. And it stems from a deep-rooted tradition of guys doing the asking. It's not just an Asian issue, either. Julia's always saying she'll never ask a guy out on a date. She's even less likely to propose to a partner. She simply couldn't. Why? Because she's the fairer sex and of a much more sensitive disposition. Society thinks if a girl rejects a guy, he'll happily move on to the next hot object (and I'm sure this is true in most cases). If a guy rejects a girl, we're talking deep melancholy and hand wringing akin to Lady Macbeth.

So while us girls get dolled up and go to these events, we rarely talk to any boys. It's expected that they'll spot us, make some enquiries to find out who we are, only to realise that we're not really looking, as that's what we tell everyone when asked. We're just here for the charity, we say. Oh and to make some friends.

Very few admirable friends of mine have actually bucked this trend and when meeting new people, they offer up their unmarried status and ask if they know anyone who's single. Reena did this when she attended our mutual friend's wedding last year. I almost did a slow clap. Reena is a legend. She isn't waiting for someone to fall into her lap. She knows life isn't like that, sometimes you have to make your own fairy-tale. She always tells me, the wider you cast your net, the more people you ask, then the more people know you are looking, which increases your chances of finding 'the one' in this big old world.

As for me, I'm not quite sure if I'll attend another 'charity' event. A big downfall for me is the buffet meal. Put me in front of a buffet and I WILL get my money's worth. This means two rounds of chicken tikka, a load of biryani and three (small) kebabs, which isn't the most attractive sight to any potential suitor.

Having said that, it does seem that despite its drawbacks, these fundraisers may be a source of eligible men. In fact, I may have already secured one...

# 10<sup>th</sup> June, The tease

Something doesn't feel right.

Heena hasn't got back to me about the pharmacist. It's been two months now, so she probably never will.

I messaged her after the event, saying how good it was to meet her and that I hoped we could grab a coffee soon. I didn't even ask about the pharmacist as that would seem far too keen. She didn't reply. I thought you only played hard to get with someone you want to date. Either Heena's very busy, or can't be bothered. I chose to believe she's busy.

A few days later, she gave a generic response about how she's sorry for the late reply but it was great meeting me and we should grab coffee soon. No mention of the pharmacist. For a girl who was so quick to read between the lines and draw out my hunting status, she sure didn't take the hint about why I *really* got in touch.

Two weeks passed without hearing from her. I was debating whether to send her another message to set up a coffee date. Navigating this new friendship seemed like harder work than an actual relationship. I text her again, about something else entirely. True to form, she took a few days to respond and still didn't mention the pharmacist.

What was my next move? I had no freaking idea.

That's one thing I really hate about these half-arsed matchmakers - they're really half-arsed. I didn't ask HER if she knew anyone. She approached ME. She probed into my single status, said that she knew someone and promised feedback.

I finally bumped into her at another 'charity' event. Yep, I gave it another go. I arranged to meet Sophia and her husband there. Upon arrival, I spotted Heena so went over to say hello.

"Hey stranger," she said. "Where have you been hiding? I haven't seen you for ages."

*That's because you've been actively avoiding me*, I thought. But of course, my PR politeness led the conversation. "I know it's been a while. How are you?"

"I'm good but it's been crazy busy with work. I've been travelling all across the North of England and just got back from a three hour round trip to Carlisle."

"Oh wow, you have been busy. So... how was Carlisle?"

"Grim. It rained even heavier than it does in Manchester, which wasn't much fun on the motorway. And the meetings are *tough*. I spent half the time dodging awkward chats with the Asian GPs."

"How do you mean?"

"Well, put it this way, they're less interested in the drugs I'm showcasing and more fixated on me. Oh and it's *sooo* condescending." She does an exaggerated eye roll. "If I hear one more guy tell me I'm too pretty to be a rep, I'll scream." She throws her head back laughing.

This is my chance.

"Well, I bet it's nice to be chased by doctors about something not medical-related. Haven't any of them caught your eye?"

Heena sighs. "No. Well, I was speaking to someone a few weeks back but it turned out he wasn't ready for marriage. And

as for the GPs, if they can't take me seriously as a professional working woman, I can't take them seriously as a prospective
husband."

"That's a shame, sometimes quantity doesn't bring quality,"
I chip in.

"Oh it rarely does. At least not in my case. I'm thinking if I
hit 30 and I'm still single, I might even have to... look online."
She does a fake shudder.

Heena doesn't probe into my non-existent love life and
instead glances over my shoulder. She's looking for an escape
plan. I bite the bullet. "So what happened to that guy you mentioned? What was he? A pharmacist, or something?"

She barely conceals a wicked smile. "Oh yeah... him. Well,
I'm just taking my time to find out more about him. I know
you're a nice girl, so I want to make sure he's a decent guy. I
figured I'd do some Facebook research first to see if he's got a
dodgy past, or if he's had many girlfriends before."

I never knew Facebook was the window to someone's soul.
Heena promised to stalk his social media the last time we met.

Then she surprises me. "Don't make it obvious but he's actually here tonight."

"Where?" I almost shout, making it very obvious.

Heena raises a finger to her red-painted full lips: "Ssh... he's
literally right behind you, in that group of guys and girls. He's
the tall one wearing a hound's-tooth blazer."

She had me at tall. I try to turn around subtly to see who
this mythical pharmacist is. I spot him. He's actually quite
good-looking, with fair skin, sharp features and charcoal-black
eyes. He looks more Pakistani than Bengali (it's no secret that
Bengali boys are often short and dark, with some exceptions).

I also have to applaud his snappy dress sense. Black and white hound's tooth is something I rarely see in suit form. It's usually the reserve of women's winter coats.

Given that we're no more than two metres apart, I'm wondering why she doesn't just introduce us. I'm also wishing I had the balls to request an introduction. However, a lifetime of being indoctrinated into thinking the guy should do all the work holds me back from being so assertive. I also don't want Heena to think I'm a floozy.

"Leave it with me. Once I've checked him out, I'll get back to you. But I'm just going to say hi to some people I know, so I'll see you later."

Just like that, she leaves me hanging to join a gaggle of identikit friends – girls who are also in their late twenties and still doing this fake charity thing. My gut instinct is usually right. It was telling me she wouldn't come good but I kind of held false hope. And he's handsome.

I'm not sure what to do. I'd love to somehow segue a conversation with him. He's currently cornered by three hair-flicking, floozy-esque girls. I see him scanning the room and our eyes meet for a brief moment. He does a half smile, before looking away. Or maybe that was in my head? He walks away from his groupies, heading towards the buffet. This is my chance. Should I go over? If it were a business-networking event, this would be so much easier. I'd have an excuse to speak to him. But in this forum, where everyone's single and judging, I couldn't just approach him. Or could I?

I figure I should look my best anyway, so I head to the ladies room to touch up my lipstick. But before I get there, I feel a tap on my shoulder.

Is this my moment? Is the pharmacist approaching *me*? I turn around.

Of course he's not. This isn't a Bollywood movie. It's Sophia and who I assume to be her husband, Adnan. I'm glad to see them, as I no longer have to loiter around by myself. But I'm also disappointed and embarrassed that I thought for a second that the fit pharmacist had singled me out. I glance over at the buffet. He's still there, loading up on kebabs.

Sophia and her husband are two people I would never have put together. It's like Beauty and the Beast. She is petite and pretty, like a human Bambi, with the long eyelashes to boot. Adnan is more of a gentle giant sort. Very tall, heavy set, balding and bespectacled, with a hooked nose. He looks down through his glasses, seemingly in judgment. Though he's also a bit of a contradiction, as his stern face is in stark contrast with his lavender jumper. Maybe Sophia made him dress summery.

He looks at me with a mischievous smirk. "So have you spotted any boys you like the look of?"

I'm slightly flustered by the question.

Sophia butts in: "Don't embarrass her. I told you, best behaviour on your first meeting."

"Oh, come on. I'm asking because that's why we're here... to wingman you. Or maybe that should be wing-couple. Well, Sophia has an ulterior motive. She's here to protect me from all the women who fling themselves at my feet as soon as I enter the door."

Laughing, Sophia says in her high-pitched, shrill tone: "Oi! I think it's the other way round, doll face."

"Ignore my jealous wife. But seriously, any boys of interest?"

I gasp in mock shock, as he seems the jokey sort. "How very dare you! I'm not that kind of girl. I'm just here to raise money."

"Pah! I've heard that before. Even Sophia and I aren't just here for the Syrian refugees. We want to make new friends. We're getting sick of each other."

I really like this couple. They have the fun dynamic I'd like to have when I get married. Despite my shallow first impression, I now get what Sophia sees in him. I contemplate telling them about the pharmacist. It's much easier for Adnan to approach him and then I can muscle my way into a conversation. But I leave it, hoping Heena will get back to me as promised.

Adnan scans the room and fixes his gaze on the pharmacist. "What about that guy there? He's brave with his check jacket, I'll give him that. Few guys can pull that off."

I'm not sure what to say. "I'm not taking part in your matchmaking experiment. And I don't want to be introduced to anyone right now. The only date I'm interested in is with the buffet."

That was a good one. I'm silently applauding myself.

"But you are looking to meet someone, right?"

Not this again. Sophia shoots a look at Adnan as if to say, *leave it*.

"Honestly, I'm cool. Like I say, it's me and the samosas tonight."

He holds up his hands in defence. "It's your choice. Sorry if I'm being pushy. I'm just insisting because I know it's hard for girls to do the asking, or even admit they're looking. Most girls tend to hide behind shyness. Or... humour. It would be much easier for us guys if you ladies were just straight up."

That was a bit close to the bone.

Sophia, sensing my discomfort and seeing my face change, interjects: "OK Sigmund Freud, you can leave your psychoanalyst hat at home. Sorry hon, he always wanted to be a shrink but never made the grade."

I laugh. "It's OK. I appreciate the effort and I'll let you both know if I need a wingman."

The three of us hang out together for another hour. I raid the buffet and then head home, back to my parents semi-detached house that's claustrophobic with its lack of privacy.

Mum probes me on the event before I even get to take my shoes off. "How was your thing? What was it again?"

"A charity event for Syrian refugees."

"Mash Allah that's good. I help them too. I give £50 on Bangla channel today as the mesaab was raising money. So, were there lots of people there?" Mum asks.

I'm really not in the mood for this. "Yes, quite a few. Look mum, I'm just going to get changed and catch the 10 o'clock news."

As I head upstairs, mum quizzes me on what she *really* wants to know. "Were there any Bangla people there?"

"Not many. Maybe one or two. It's more of an event frequented by Pakistanis. Then again, there are more Pakistanis than Bengalis in Manchester anyway."

"Yes, that shame. Were most people married, or single there?"

"Seemed to be more singles, from what I saw."

"And what about among the Ban-galis?"

"Same."

Mum leans in over the off-white bannister. "Were there single boys?"

"Well the host was definitely single."

"Oh. What does he do? Was he your age?"

"No. Much older."

"Really?"

"Yes mum, really. People much older than me are still single. This guy probably had a decade on me."

"What? Noooo... I don't buleev! What's happening to people these days? Old and crusty and not yet married. When do they expect to have kids?"

"Mum! I don't know. I don't know. But you know what happens when I miss the news. There'll always be a headline story that involves my bloody sector so I need to be in the loop."

In truth I caught the news at six and the healthcare sector is thankfully scandal-free but I desperately wanted to get away from this interrogation. I didn't want mum to think that there are eligible boys in my midst that I'm unable to charm.

However, if I thought the questions would end there, I was wrong. Little sis makes the rare effort of looking up from her phone when I enter our room.

"How come *you're* home so late?"

SINCE THE EVENT, HEENA'S barely been in contact. I think that ship has sailed. Or it was never a ship in the first place. It was a bloody dinghy that sunk along with my hopes of being set up with a handsome pharmacist.

This brings me nicely onto my rant of the day. Why do women do this to each other? If you indeed do 'know someone', why don't you pursue it properly and help a sister out? If the guy turns out to be a loser, we won't hold it against you. But we *will* begrudge you for giving us false hope.

Julia once said that women are each other's worst enemies and this proves that she's right. With women, there's a real sense of competition. There are fewer men in the world, so naturally pickings are slim. I don't think Heena wanted the pharmacist for herself. She's Pakistani, I'm Bengali and so we're going for men of different ethnic origins. However, I don't think she was particularly bothered about helping me find a partner, as she had to sort herself out first.

From a cynical point of view, I wonder whether she was just teasing and slightly enjoying me chasing her. However, I'd like to think better of her. Maybe because it wasn't her problem, she simply couldn't be bothered. She suggested someone flippantly but didn't care enough to follow it through. But this is in fact just as mean as my first, more cynical, theory.

Us women can be bitches. Total bitches. Sometimes we just don't want to see other girls happy, unless we are happy ourselves. Jane Austen's *Emma* might have enjoyed matchmaking despite being single herself but in real life there aren't many like her.

I think another lesson from this situation is that I shouldn't get my hopes up too soon. I've always been a glass half empty kind of girl. Somewhere along the line I learnt that if I assume the worst, I won't be disappointed. This is a mantra I adopted at university. I'd be on the pessimistic side about exam outcomes. And in my career, I'd always play down job interviews, assuming I wasn't in the running until I actually got the job. Some may think that this is a fucked up logic but it worked for me. So far, every time I've dared to dream, I've been put back in my place with disappointment.

However, there is an inner struggle. Despite being glass half empty in most aspects of my life, when it comes to boys and marriage, the inner romantic in me is battling it out with my cynical self. Deep down, I'm about as Bollywood as they come. After one meeting, I'll tell myself not to get excited but in my heart, I'm planning my wedding and picturing my world coming together with a perfect stranger. You might think that's a bit obsessive - and it is - but I think there's a bit of a fantasist in all us women. We so badly want to find Mr Right that we may shoehorn Mr Wrong to fit that mould. Or, in my case, Mr I-know-nothing-about-but-I'm-still-excited.

Despite my best intentions, I pinned my hopes on this person who someone had fleetingly suggested and I'd never properly met. Perhaps this was down to the fact that there isn't much talent out there. Regardless, I need to get my head out of the clouds.

From now on, I'm not going to get my hopes up about anyone until there's a sparkly rock on my finger. I will assume the worst, keep my glass half empty and silence my inner Bollywood heroine.

# 16<sup>th</sup> June, A rishtaa

Whatever people say about arranged marriages, one thing's for certain - we don't mess around. No sooner was I done mourning the pharmacist I saw once and never spoke to, than a suitor has come my way.

They say that nothing mends a broken heart like falling in love again. With the arranged marriage process, nothing helps you get over someone you've never met, like the prospect of being matched up with someone else you've never met. In this case, it's my first rishtaa, who is coming next weekend.

A rishtaa is basically a potential suitor who comes to meet the girl's family. The boy comes with his parents, they all have a chat and size each other up. If both sides are happy with what they see, the boy and girl can meet again a few times, both formally and on the sly, to get to know each other. If they're still keen, then they have a match. It's as simple as that.

Aunty Fatima (who isn't actually my auntie but is too old for me to call her by name) knows a boy who is looking to get married and thinks we'd suit each other pretty well. I always find these recommendations funny. My parents have been looking for a suitable boy for months now, so why didn't Aunty Fatima mention this guy before? Or has the boy's family only just mentioned that their son is ready to settle down? Either way, mum got pretty excited and I did a little, too. We swapped pictures and biodata and decided we liked what we saw so arranged a meeting.

I'm also glad that my pictures in the park came good in the end.

I want to be all glass half empty. I won't get excited... but... my rishtaa (not that I'm marking my territory) is 5ft 10in, which is practically gargantuan for a Bengali boy. He works in IT and is the middle child of three. This is the perfect placement in the family tree, as the oldest usually shoulders the initial financial burden and parental pressure, while the youngest is left to take care of the folks once the elder siblings have flown the nest. Nobody really troubles the middle child. So I'm thinking I'm onto a winner.

While I wouldn't say he's drop dead gorgeous, he's got what my mum would describe as a 'nice face'. He's got kind eyes and a broad, warm smile. Also, I don't know if it's because of the contrast with his dark skin but his teeth are really white. I'm talking Hollywood white. So if we ended up getting hitched I'd probably have to visit the hygienist for a deep clean on a regular basis.

The impending rishtaa event is like the Bengali equivalent of a state visit. Everyone needs to be present for the occasion, including my two older sisters who have long flown the nest and their respective children.

Mum reels off the boy's details over the phone to my eldest sister and gets me to send a screenshot of the boy's photo and CV to my more computer-savvy middle sister. My eldest sister, who had an arranged marriage back home in Bangladesh, is impressed with his height but has one slight reservation. "He's a bit on the dark side. But never mind, it's not like you're particularly fair or anything."

Big sis has this unique gift for sharing an opinion on something or someone else, while shitting on me at the same time. It's quite poetic. She's 13 years older than me and it's like a generational difference. Big sis was born in Bangladesh but mum and dad moved to the UK before she was three. Yet she acts like she's spent her whole life back home. She's more of the old guard – like my mum's generation where feelings are repressed and you call a spade a spade. Or in my case, you tell me I'm dark-skinned – which is highly undesirable for a Bengali girl - and expect me to suck it up.

Middle sister - always the comedian – has a great response when she receives the rishtaa photo: "Lucky you, he's bleedin' gorgeous."

That's a famous line from the film East is East, where the hilarious neighbour comes to check out the mono-browed, bucktoothed rishtaa that has come for Mr Khan's very westernised son. I don't think she's being sarcastic. But I don't think she's swooning over my rishtaa either. She's just being her funny, random self. Middle sis got married eight years ago – at 24 - to a boy from Bradford.

Initially mum thought it might be better for her to get married back home like my eldest sister. Courtesy of my brother-in-law, big sis speaks perfect Bengali, has raised bi-lingual kids, goes back home every summer and cooks a mean fish curry. With her husband's family back in Bangladesh, big sister never had to live with the in-laws – thus avoiding any potential conflict that can occur when sharing a home (and crucially a kitchen) with another family.

However, middle sister was adamant that she wanted to get married to a boy from the UK. Someone that could, quite literally, speak her language and be on her wavelength. And her desire for a UK-born husband turned out well, as she's happily married with two kids. Her husband is a bit of an Asian wide-boy, with his side job of selling cars alongside his main occupation as a teacher but we love him all the same. Most importantly, my sister loves him too. Mum's concerns were also unfounded – Middle sis lived with her in-laws for the first two years of marriage but they were so taken by her trophy-bride beauty that they didn't care that she couldn't cook curry. She's got a great relationship with them to this day and thank goodness for that. If her marriage didn't work out, mum and dad would probably be looking for a Bangladesh-based rishtaa for me.

I remember when middle sis was going through the arranged marriage process. Scores of rishtaa photos came through our letterbox. Many of which were offensive to the eyes, or were accompanied by pompous biodatas. And boy, did we laugh. One thing I learnt from that time is that humour is essential. Humour gets you through the awkwardness. Humour gets you through the heartache. And at the end of it all, when a rishtaa doesn't turn into a marriage, funny is all you have left. Luckily for us brownies, the modernised arranged marriage provides shit loads of comedy material.

After my sisters are told about the rishtaa, mum shares the boy's biodata with dad. In true dad style, he takes one look, does a fake cough and then says: "Yes, yes, well as long as you think he's ok," before returning to reading his newspaper. Poor dad, he's the last to be consulted. I sometimes wonder whether he wishes he had a son, as he's both outnumbered and out of the loop in a family of women.

The whole informing the elders' bit is more of a formality, as parents believe it's important to keep the 'inner circle' involved. This is to ensure that nobody feels left out of the party. The last thing I want to do is risk ruffling feathers by making my possible marriage nobody's business but my own.

Clearly mum and dad don't trust me, or even themselves, to form an opinion on this boy. The more people that meet him the better, they say. *Spread the blame*, they secretly think. I don't think they've heard the analogy of too many cooks spoiling the broth.

But I do *kind of* get their logic. Who I will marry is the biggest decision of my life, so they want to do everything they can to help me make sure it's the right one. And in their view, garnering trusted opinions would help build their confidence. If everyone likes this boy, he's probably OK. If nobody does, chances are he's a knob.

My white friends and nosey work colleagues may balk at this concept but I see examples of getting approval from 'the pack' every single day.

For example, my boss Maggie has a terrible track record of keeping hold of her staff. And I can see why. When I joined the company, I spent the first few weeks shitting myself daily (not literally of course). Maggie was intimidating, snappy and didn't suffer fools. But once I proved myself with my press release writing prowess - I broke her steely veneer to find that she's actually kind of nice. Not everyone got that far.

Before I joined the team and became her star pupil, there was a revolving door of young PR execs that had left in tears, tantrums or with a bout of workplace stress. One guy even threw in the towel on his third day and did the professional thing of just not turning up. Ever again.

When it came to recruitment and retention, Maggie had form. Bad form. So when she needed a new account manager, she was determined to get it right. And how would she do this? With a thorough one-to-one interview? No. A watertight competency-based test? No. Working on her gut instinct? Don't be silly.

Maggie was better than that. When it came to interviews, she spread the load. She made a chosen few of us come in, one by one, and speak to the candidates. We weren't briefed on what to ask. It wasn't formal. We were just sent in to suss them out. Then Maggie would ask us what we thought of each interviewee. Based on our opinions, Maggie chose her manager.

We all knew what she was doing. She didn't want to decide alone. She was sharing the blame. And it was genius.

In the oh-so-progressive world of the UK dating scene (you know, the land of the free where us darkies live), the same thing happens all the time. During her training contract, a fellow trainee relentlessly pursued Julia. She half-fancied him but before she accepted his 100th invitation for a drink, she roped me and some other trusted confidantes into rocking up at one of her after-work drinks to help make an informed choice on Martin. FYI, Martin couldn't stop talking about money, which rubbed all of us up the wrong way. Not least Julia, who comes from an old fashioned have-it-but-don't-talk-about-it family. He never stood a chance.

People always seek the seal of approval before taking the next step. They meet the parents before deciding to move in together. They go to a family wedding before proposing. Whichever way you look at it, getting hitched is often a group decision by proxy. Yes, sometimes love defies the odds and people get together despite waves of disapproval. But from what I've seen, that rarely ends well. If you're still in doubt, just look at Romeo and Juliet.

No matter what your culture, you want your tribe to like your guy. My parents are no different. Except it's my potential guy, not theirs.

IF YOU'VE EVER SEEN pictures of the Queen entertaining at Buckingham Palace, you'll know that no state visit is complete without a carefully chosen outfit. I mean, do you think Kate Middleton just wakes up, grabs her nearest tiara, puts on whichever frock doesn't need ironing and legs it to the stateroom at Buckingham Palace? Of course not. Each sartorial choice is meticulously curated.

I don't have a tiara and my salwar kameez collection is less couture and more closing down sale (saree shops *always* have closing down sales, though they never actually close down). With this in mind, mum decides that I need a new outfit, or three. We head to Rusholme, Manchester's Indian high street, where we have a piss-poor selection of saree shops, too many kebab places and a halal cash and carry. Mum reasons that it's a convenient time to go outfit shopping as we need to restock our freezer with chicken, so we can kill two birds with one stone. She may be rubbish with a camera but she multitasks like a boss.

Asian outfits aren't my general uniform. I have this unwritten rule – I reserve Asian clothes for Eid, weddings and occasional house wear (some of the cotton tunics are *ever so* comfy). But for facing the outside world, it's jeans, dresses and tops all the way. Because God forbid, my attire should give away my ethnicity.

Plus, I always find Asian clothes shopping to be something of an ordeal, hence my limited selection. Many shops don't have adequate changing rooms and you're expected to make a purchase based on just touching the material or holding the outfit up against yourself. Often you end up with buyer's remorse. Once you get home, the trousers are too short, or the dress is too long. Or that specific shade of aubergine that looked great under the shop's bright lights, doesn't do your complexion any favours in real life.

And then there's the haggling. Oh my, this is where it can get ugly. I've seen slanging matches because the shopkeeper refused to knock £10 from the asking price of a £300 outfit.

Customers have left shops red-faced and flustered from bartering. It makes the General Election's televised leadership debate appear tame. Neither side will budge from their price. Then the customer pulls out the big guns – they walk away. Slowly though, leaving just enough time to give the shopkeeper a chance to call them back and negotiate one last deal. But sometimes, calling their bluff doesn't work. There have been times when I've threatened to leave. And then I started walking. And continued walking...

Each side has to suss out the other. The shopkeeper asks when you need the outfit and what the occasion is. You never, ever tell them you need it soon, or for a special occasion. Otherwise they'll know you're desperate and won't give you much of a discount. So you have to pretend you're buying a sparkly number just to wear around the house at some point in the distant future. As you do.

If this sounds like something of a strategic battle, you'd be right. Reluctantly, I head into the trenches with mum.

She's the first source of conflict, as we have glaringly different tastes when it comes to choosing the perfect outfit.

"This one's pretty," she says, holding up a pink leopard print number.

Bless her, she doesn't know that leopard print has risqué connotations in the western world. Plus the outfit is ugly as hell. The problem is, dressing for my mum and dressing for a potential husband are two very different things. Mum doesn't get this. I rubbish her choice and instead turn my attention to a simple beige number. It's understated and elegant.

"That might make you lit-ool bit... daaark." Mum bites her lip, as she clearly feels mean reminding me – yet again - of my brown disposition. "How about this, it's *much* nicer and looks fit for a special occasion?"

I examine her suggestion. It is a grand number, with delicate stone embroidery intertwined with gold thread work. It's also got a princely price tag to boot. Given that I'll probably only wear it once or twice before it goes out of fashion, I'm mindful of the cost per wear. When I tell mum this, she's not happy.

"You're so stingy. You're earning enough to buy decent clothes. Look at what other girls wear. They're probably on half your money."

"We've not all got expensive taste like you, mum. With your M&S Greek Style yoghurt-buying ways."

We both stifle a laugh at mum's spendthrift nature. But it's true, she does buy her yoghurt from M&S. And unlike me, she rarely shops in the sale.

The last shop we visit smells more like a restaurant than a boutique clothes store, with the strong scent of daal permeating the mannequin-filled space. The shop man must be on a working lunch break, though there's technically no such thing. He mops up his daal with a roti before looking up to see us. We head out to leave but he says: "No, come, come, sisters. I finished," as he grabs a wet wipe for his haldi-stained hands.

Among the row of dolls lining the walls in colourful salwar kameezes, I spy a faux silk gold and pink number. Mum's not too happy about the length of the kameez, so I hold it against myself to show her that it's not too short. I win this battle. Like all the outfits in the shop and in fact along this whole high street, it doesn't come with a price tag. The shop man tells us there's a multi-buy deal where you can get the exact same outfit in a different colour at a discount. Handy, if this rishtaa doesn't work out and I have to do this all over again.

Having had his meal interrupted, the shop man wants to make it worth his while by charging £75 for both outfits. This is way more than they're worth. Despite my M&S loving mum's insistence on outspending my budget, she agrees with me and wants to feel like we've got the better end of the deal.

The haggling game begins:

Mum: "That's not worth £75."

Shop man: "Sister, this is quality material. Touch it."

The material is harsh to the touch, certainly not silky smooth.

Mum: "Brother come on, £75 is far too much for two simple outfits. Please reduce price."

I should point out that mum and the shop man aren't actually siblings.

Shop man (shaking his head): "No, no, no. We can't go any lower. This is already a discounted price."

Mum: "Come on brother, we'll take them both for £45."

Shop man (fake gasping): "Sister! That is an insult. That's below cost price! I couldn't go any lower than... £60."

Me: "What about £50?"

Mum elbows me in the ribs and mumbles in Bengali that I shouldn't get involved. The shop guy is Indian so doesn't understand her words but her actions transcend any language. After doing this bartering dance for what seems like an eternity, we settle on £50, which is what I suggested originally.

Outfit sorted. Family members briefed. Roll on weekend.

# 21<sup>st</sup> June, Tall-boy, small talk

It seems like the rishtaa and his family are downstairs for ages and I haven't even been summoned yet. I hear muffled chat and oil frying in the kitchen. That means mum underestimated her samosa count and is replenishing supplies. I suspect we'll need at least two dozen as the boy is accompanied by his mum, dad, sister-in-law and sister. His family believe in safety in numbers, just like mine.

My poor mum, she must be getting all flustered with all the last-minute cooking but I hope she's factored in my portion. I think I deserve at least three samosas after being held hostage in my own room.

My youngest niece, who is four, comes upstairs to see me. She looks adorable in her mint green salwar kameez with harem pants. She's even got matching bangles. She might be teeny but I can already tell she'll be as geisha-like as her mum.

I ask her to sneak me a samosa from the kitchen.

Excited to be burdened with such responsibility, she rushes downstairs and shouts: "Nani, auntie wants a samosa!"

So much for being covert.

I hear mum shush and shoo her out of the kitchen, whispering terribly audibly: "Shomsha come later! She not starve up there."

I'm guessing that as a delicate prospective bride-to-be, it shouldn't be known that I eat.

It's moments like this that I realise how crap I am with killing time. Sitting idly just doesn't sit well (pun intended). As I wait upstairs, I realize that this is one of the rare moments I am completely by myself. Usually my teenage sister is sat on the next bed, in her own world on her phone. In this prolonged solitude, I actually miss having her to moan at. Bloody ironic. I add another layer - or three - of pressed powder. I must be careful, as my biggest beauty mistake is an over-done face.

I never really got an explanation from mum as to why I have to wait upstairs when a rishtaa arrives. It's just the done thing. I have my own theory about it... I *think* the idea is that the rishtaa and his family only get to see you for a brief while, so they only see the best of you. Like the trailer for a movie. Short and sweet, so you get the idea and can decide if you want to see more.

I'm also thinking that an exclusive sneak peek means that there's less time for me to eff up, speak out of turn, or commit any other social faux pas, like picking my nose. Because that's *obviously* what I do in polite company, right?

I don't recall how it worked with my eldest sister but I remember my middle sister would wait upstairs until summoned when she had rishtaa visits. She'd only come downstairs briefly, sit and chat with the prospective in-laws and then disappear upstairs again. Kind of like an enigma, a brown Keyser Soze, if you will. This air of mystery suited middle sis. She's fair-skinned, graceful and perfected the geisha walk for each boy that visited (and there were quite a few, though not quite on a par with my cousin Rashda's number).

I'm not sure if I can pull off the same mystique, as I'm more of a treader than a dainty tip-toe type. Plus I'll be wearing heels.

And we have shiny laminate flooring. While this will be the first time I'm allowed to wear heels indoors, I'm guessing I'll be noisy and stompy.

Finally, my eldest sister, the most traditional of us daughters, comes upstairs armed with a glass of water. She's enrobed her curvy size-16 figure in a pink, jewel-encrusted saree and has accessorised with the necklace that's part of her wedding gold. She is never knowingly underdressed. I'm also not sure if she got the memo that this is *my* rishtaa meeting, not hers.

Supportive as ever, she tells me my makeup is too cake-y. I knew the third layer of powder was a bit much. I ask her to bring me a samosa, which she refuses as she says it'll ruin my lipstick. She tells me I can eat when I'm downstairs, though we both know that's a lie. If I can't eat a samosa in the privacy of my own room, I sure as shit won't be able to chow done on one in front of my potential future husband. Plus the last thing I want is for him to see me with crumbs around my mouth.

Escorted by big sis, I head downstairs for a date with destiny. But not before she whispers a parting shot: "Your kameez is too short. Let me pull it down a bit."

It's a bit bloody late to tell me that now and no amount of yanking will make a thigh-skimming number long and flowy.

As I enter our living room, trying to tread more quietly, the first new face I see is who I presume to be the boy's mum (unless father time hasn't been kind to his sister). Straight away I feel uneasy. She doesn't look like the friendliest old gal in the world. After a brief glance in my direction, her small, deep-set eyes look unimpressed. As I sit down, I tug at the hemline of my sequin-adorned kameez, scratching my fingers on the harshly cut embellishments. Maybe it is a bit short. I can't quite figure out if the mum's disappointed upon seeing me, or she just has a permanent resting bitch face. Whatever it is, it's making me nervous and my nervous face isn't good. When I'm not smiling, I tend to sport a scowl by default. Unwittingly, the mum and I are having a resting bitch face-off.

I have a niggling feeling that she may have seen my elegant middle sis and been disappointed when I came downstairs, heels almost cracking the laminate. I must remember to tell mum not to invite middle sis to any other rishtaa meetings.

Anyway, to say it's awkward is an understatement. The first few minutes seem like hours. Mum solicits an ice-breaker in the only way she knows: "Have some shomsha," she says with a smile.

I look down at my small plate, which has four perfectly formed golden crispy triangles. Usually the heady smell of oil, spice and keema would be enough to make me devour the plate. Not this time. I'm too nervous to eat.

Thankfully, the boy's sister and sister-in-law enter the room. They must have been in the kitchen chatting to middle sis. His sister-in-law is very pretty, with delicate, fair, China-doll features. She's incredibly petite and looks like a young girl in her blue saree.

His sister, in contrast, is tall, slightly broad and darker skinned. She seems friendly and smiley and we fall into conversation on the standard safe topic of work. She works in recruitment and once she asks me what I do, I relish the opportunity to talk about my main bragging right. I launch into how I get clients in the media by working with journalists and writing press releases. I name-drop that I've met Fergie, the Duchess of York, at a PR event. I can talk at length about my work. I'm impressed with how well I've done for myself, as my career is one area where I've surpassed my older sisters, who were both married before their work-life had a chance to get off the ground.

Middle sis eyeballs me. Her look suggests that I'm waffling on about myself too much. So I ask his sister a follow-up question about her work, even though I'm not really interested in the answer. Recruitment bores me to death.

The boy's dad is then summoned to see me. He seems much nicer than his wife. He's got a round, open, friendly face and a thick black moustache. Both son and daughter take after their dark-skinned dad. He's got a bigger nose and ears than his children but I think that's just due to ageing. His dad shares an anecdote of how he met my dad on a flight to Bangladesh years ago. He mumbles something about how this is meant to be. So while the miserable mum seems miffed, I think I've won over the dad.

Suddenly the room fills with a masculine, musty fragrance. I think it's Tom Ford. I feel my overly powdered face turn warm as the boy walks in (boys offer sneak previews, too). He looks even taller than his 5ft 10 stats and is broad shouldered. He's as dark-skinned in person as his photo suggests but that's OK, as I'll seem fair in comparison. He's dressed for the occasion, in a smart black well-fitted suit with a crisp white shirt. I'm so used to seeing Bengali boys in ill-fitting suits of an unusual hue at weddings (think petrol blue), that Tall-boy's effort is appreciated.

I'm not sure what to do. I imagine hearing mum's photographer voice in my ear saying *smile but not too much*. So I try out a wry smile – nothing too toothy – but I imagine this makes me look slightly constipated, so I revert to my default non-smiling scowl. I don't know where to look. I can't make it obvious that I'm checking him out, so I have to do princess Diana-like furtive glances. I'm not very good at this.

My big sister initiates the ice-breaker this time, asking Tall-boy, in Bengali: "Have you been to Bangladesh?"

I told you she was old school.

He says he last visited when he was 15. My previous trip was when I was 13, so we went there in the same year. Wait a minute, were we on the same flight that his dad mentioned? Maybe we are meant to be.

I'm unprepared for the next bit. Everyone clears the room, while my mum whispers to me: "You two talk to each other."

Mum doesn't even make eye contact when she says this. Despite having gone through this rishtaa process numerous times with my older sisters, she still finds it as cringe worthy as I do. Tall-boy and I are left to it. He keeps ruffling his thick, shiny hair. I can tell he's a little nervous. It's kind of cute.

I initiate a conversation, smiling as I look towards our beige and brown paisley-print curtain.

Me: "So... this is a bit awkward."

Tall-boy: "I know. Have you done many of these before?"

Wow! Isn't that the brown equivalent of asking how many boyfriends you've had?

I can see in the corner of my eye that he's looking directly at me but I don't make eye contact. I'm not really sure what today's rishtaa etiquette is but I've always thought the girl assumes the coy role. He then lowers his eyes to our anonymous-looking laminate floor. Crap, there's a dust-covered hairball, trapped between our brown fur rug and the shiny laminate.

Mum must have missed it when she was hoovering this morning. She must have been rushing, as she's normally so thorough.

Me: "No, it's my first time."

Tall-boy: "Mine too."

I bet he's lying.

Me: "Do you think our parents are listening behind the door?"

Tall-boy: "Probably. I wouldn't put it past my mum."

We both do a fake laugh. But we stifle our pretend giggles so our parents - who are undoubtedly eavesdropping - don't think we're flirting on the first meeting.

Tall-boy: "So what do you do when you're not working?"

Shit. This is where I wish I had some hobbies of note, like lacrosse or something. I'm not part of a sports team and I don't travel (I'd like to but mum says I can go travelling with my husband once I'm married). When I meet my few Asian friends from University, the main thing we do is eat out and talk about how hard it is to get married. When I meet my non-Asian friends, we eat out and moan about boys in general. Anyway, I best keep those hobbies to myself.

Me: "I like to eat out. I also love to go to the cinema."

Tall-boy: "Oh cool, me too. What's the last film you've seen?"

The door opens and big sis walks in. Saved by the bell. I've never been so happy to see an overdressed saree-clad woman in my life. I haven't been to the cinema in years. I can't remember the last film I watched. It was probably a *Bridget Jones* sequel, which shows how long it's been. But I lied, as I didn't want to say the only thing I do in my spare time is eat and bitch.

Our two-minute chat was the grand finale of the event. Tall-boy and his convoy of relatives pile out, while his dad stays back and speaks to my dad, who is dwarfed next to him. I notice that my dad's decked out in his best outfit too, a grey flecked salwar kameez and prayer hat. He looks like the cutest of garden gnomes. Tall-boy's dad says something about being in touch. He's obviously keen.

As they leave, big sis closes the door and clasps her bangle-adorned hands together in glee. "Well, I think that went rather well, don't you?"

I try hard to keep a straight face, as I don't want to show my excitement. But I can't help but grin. "We'll see."

TONIGHT I'LL SLEEP well. The whole experience was much more nerve-wracking than I expected. I am knackered, excited and hopeful. The adrenalin build-up, combined with feeling more nervous than I'd expected, has left me drained. I knew rishtaa meetings were formal but I wasn't prepared for how emotionally exhausting the process would be. It was like going for the biggest job interview of my life.

Yes, I got made up just like I do when I go to my pretend charity events. I wore a gold, delicately jewelled salwaar kameez (one of my double deal buys) just like I do when I go to a wedding. But this was more. So much more. This was a meeting that could change my life. While I usually breeze through situations with dry wit, I couldn't blag this one.

The worst bit was being eyeballed by his mum, as I couldn't read her. I'm not sure if she didn't like me, or just looks like a smacked-arse. On the plus side, the dad was nice. And while our chat was brief, I got a good vibe from Tall-boy. So I'm looking forward to seeing him again, in less formal circumstances.

As I go to sleep, I'm trying to silence my inner-Bollywood romantic and stop picturing Tall-boy and I getting married. *Don't get overexcited... stop getting overexcited... glass half empty...* I whisper under my breath. But it's hard not to feel optimistic.

# 13th July, Stone-cold silence

How long do you wait before realising someone's not interested? How many times do you nag your mum about whether she's heard back from a boy's family? At what point does it become shamefully desperate?

I've talked about the positives of arranged marriages, now here's the shit bit. In fact, it's the shit bit of matchmaking in general, arranged or not... the waiting and not knowing.

As far as I knew, the rishtaa visit went well. OK, maybe his mum was a sour-face but Tall-boy and I got on (in the two minutes we spoke). His dad muttered something about destiny. Everything was pointing towards a second meeting, which would give Tall-boy and I the chance to speak more without grown-ups.

Auntie Fatima called the day after the rishtaa visit to get our feedback, telling mum that Tall-boy's family seemed keen. Or at least that's what mum told me. I anticipated talk of moving forward, of next steps. It's been two weeks now... two weeks of stone-cold silence.

Mum was getting jittery too and rang auntie Fatima. But in true prim, Bengali-polite form, she asked about everything but Tall-boy:

"Salaam-walaikum, how are you?... Oh, we're good Alhamdulillah. It's been a while and no talk so thought I'll see what you do... Nah nah, not at all... I know young children leave no time. I done, my youngest a teenager now..."

I'm listening from the other room, willing mum to address the elephant on the phone line. *Go on mum, ask about Tall-boy.*

"... Yes really? I didn't know ladies had group at the masjid on Tuesdays. Yeah, I'll go sometime, just finding time."

I walk in, hoping that my mid-twenties-single-daughter presence will be enough of a prompt for mum to do some probing.

"Cooked today?... Oh, what did you make?... I haven't made shutki in soooo so many years. Sometimes I miss but my daughters complain that smell of dried fish is too strong and will offend neighbours. My kids want to be English."

I feel like ripping the phone out of mum's hand to demand an explanation from Auntie Fatima myself. But it's too late. With a polite salaam, mum hangs up.

"Why didn't you ask what happened with that...?" Oh God, I sound desperate. "You know, with that... family."

"Who family?"

"Oh you know. The boy that came to our house."

Mum laughs awkwardly, as if I'd wanted to know what colour Auntie Fatima's knickers were. "*Hmph*, I can't ask her *thaaat*! If she's not telling, how will I ask? How look it? She think we desperate."

ANOTHER WEEK PASSED, and I'm none the wiser. Here's the tricky bit...

I've asked mum twice whether she'd heard anything further from Auntie Fatima since that last conversation. But she just does her lip-stretch-grimace thing and says her calls aren't being returned. So either:

a) Auntie Fatima is being a crappy pretend Auntie

Or

b) Tall-boy's family have fed back that they're not interested but Auntie Fatima doesn't have the heart to tell my mum.

Or

c) Auntie Fatima has already said it isn't happening but mum doesn't have the heart to tell *me* and is hoping I stop asking after a few weeks.

I know I'm not getting the whole story. Mum is the one talking to Auntie Fatima, who is the conduit between my family and Tall-boy's. It's all very confusing. And worst of all, it's out of my hands. I am a control-freak in most aspects of my life. Not being in the loop on this one is a killer.

Meanwhile my mind is doing a number on me. Should I have made more effort? Didn't I smile enough? I knew my default scowl didn't help but I was nervous. I wish I had the chance to tell him this. It's not that I was dead set on marrying this boy. Our conversation wasn't enough to deduce whether he'd make a good life partner. But I was... *hopeful*. I wanted to meet him again. And I was excited.

If my middle sister knew how I'd felt after such a short meeting, she'd piss herself laughing and rip me to shreds. "Girls reject boys. At least that's how it *should* be," is what she always says.

When it was her time to get married, that's exactly how it went down.

My big sister would be equally unimpressed if she knew my feelings. Back when I was 22 and we'd turned down that first rishtaa, I confided in her that I had rear-view syndrome. But rather than a reassuring big sisterly response, I got this: "Well it's a bit late now, lady. He was a good catch too. Your brother-in-law said he was from a nice family and you rarely know what you're getting with a boy from the UK. But we can't go back and say anything to them now. You'd look silly and desperate."

Desperate. That's a word I'm sick of hearing. Don't ask. Wait til you hear back from them. The boy's family do the chasing. You sit pretty. And never, ever, let on that you like a boy. That's just... well, you know the word. I'm not saying it again.

That's what sucks about our culture. The boy has to do the asking. His family has to visit mine. They have to make the first move, initiate the call. And if they don't? You're left in this position – rishtaa limbo. It's not fair. I can't even tell mum how frustrated I am. When I chase her about it, she tells me not to worry, there'll be plenty of other boys, plus he was too dark anyway.

"Also," she reminds me, "two words of talking and you want a marriage?"

That's where the generational divide is most obvious. In mum's time, arranged marriages were much stricter. There was precious little say in the matter for women. The family made a pragmatic decision based on biodata, leaving little room for feelings. But I'm not mum and times have changed. When it comes to something as big as a future husband, it's hard to be pragmatic. I can't. I can't turn off my feelings until things progress. It's hard not to be disappointed if things don't turn out how I would have liked.

Mum also says that there's only so much that she can chase Auntie Fatima, who isn't reciprocating. If I had it my way, I'd ring up Auntie Fatima myself. I don't really care if it's a rejection (actually I do, it would hurt my pride), or if Tall-boy has found a better offer (OK, that might sting a bit). I just want to know. Then we can all move on.

It's a funny position to be in. Mum and dad can't really pursue any other rishtaas until they've concluded this one. I'm also reluctant to go to any pretend charity events until I know what's happening with Tall-boy. I'm mindful of potentially bumping into him, as it's such a small bloody world.

White people call this ghosting, when someone suddenly cuts off all contact. It happens a lot in the world of online dating, where someone can pretend to be whoever they please and then disappear without a trace before their wife finds out. Call it what you like. It's confusing and crap. And I never want to feel like this again.

# 17<sup>th</sup> July, Claustrophobia

Why is she always here? Why? Why? Why?

Yes, it's her room as much as mine but really? Does she need to spend 90% of her time holed up on her phone?

"What are you doing?" I ask.

Little sis looks up for a millisecond to say: "Nothing," before returning to her mobile.

"Well, can you do nothing downstairs?"

"What's it to you?" she scowls.

"I just need some space. Every time I come upstairs, there you are."

She puts her headphones in. Such a fucking teenager.

"I'm serious. What are you doing? What *are* you doing? Can you just go outside for 10 minutes? There's an entire world out there while you're festering up here like some... moody emo gremlin."

"If it bothers you so much, why don't you hurry up and get married so you can leave?"

She might only be 15 but little sis stings like a bee.

Mum's all-hearing ears are never too far away. "What is this shouty-shouty sweary-sweary?"

I confront her at the bannisters. "When are you going to move her into the box room? God, I'll take the box room. I don't care! I just want my own space."

"You talking about your little sister? Now is no time to do disturb. She's got GCSEs coming up, she need focus. You've seen how hard reading she is. Always upstairs."

"You think she's studying? She's on her bloody phone!"

"No I'm not, you bitch!" Shouts little sis from our room.

Mum plays this down. "Probably she just discussing school things with her friends. Small rest she take from reading sometimes, no problem. And we need spare room. I no have other daughters? How they sleep here when they come?"

Only my family would think it appropriate to keep one room empty for siblings who stay over twice a year. And they don't all fit in there, anyway. We play human Tetris every summer and Christmas holiday, packing ourselves in like sardines.

"Anyhow, it's good you come downstairs. We're out of milk and Rashda's maa coming this evening. She sound stress. Could you get some? Maybe some fresh air help little bit and make you less garam. Cool you down."

I can't believe mum's mastery at diffusing my frustration with a domestic errand. Feeling disarmed, I agree. I bloody wish I had homework, as I'd do anything to avoid Auntie Jusna. She's ever so smug as the mother of ridiculously attractive children. She talks about my cousin Rashda like she's a precious jewel, the benchmark of Bengali beauties we should all aspire to emulate.

"Where are you going now? I've got monies for milk," mum says as I head back upstairs.

"I'm just getting changed."

"Why? What's wrong with what you're wearing?"

I glance down at my green camouflage material salwar kameez, bought by big sis on one of her many trips to

Bangladesh. It's oversized, unflattering and really shouldn't be seen. I only wear it at home as it's comfortable and I don't mind it getting smelly from mum's cooking.

"I never understand you girls. So what if someone sees you in Asian clothes? You think they won't know already you're Ban-gali from seeing your face."

Mainly because I don't want to go upstairs and see my little sis' moody teenage face, I make a rare outing dressed in a salwar kameez. I'm actually glad I've come outside. The breeze is helping cool my mood. I know I shouldn't be a knob with my sister. I'm older and wiser so should take the high ground. But oh my life, it's shit being at home sometimes. The lack of space, lack of privacy... it's too much.

I walk up the road, playing dodge the neighbours like I'm on some obstacle course. I look back at our house. A modest, bay-fronted home, just enough for a small family. I can't believe it housed us all at one point.

Dad did his best to create space with what little we had. He added a UPVC front porch, which cost thousands to install but has only provided a metre of room for us to park our shoes. Instead of any practical value, it's only helped us stand out even more as the only Asians on the street. I never understood brown people's fascination with conservatories.

There was talk of getting a loft conversion but since dad retired that rumour's stopped doing the rounds. I'm glad though, as we'd only have capacity and funds for a shitty job with short stairs and a room which would require you to bend down as you enter. It's such an Asian thing to do. Build up, down, around. Bigger, better, more PVCU.

Nobody else on the street has a conversion of any sort. They've stuck with what they started with and kept it classy. I suspect though that none of our neighbours have more than two kids. In fact, most of the people I see, who largely keep themselves to themselves, are empty nesters and retirees. We couldn't be more different but that doesn't stop us trying.

Helping us stick out further is the lack of foliage in our front garden. Despite having a decent space, we have done precisely eff all with it. While the pensioners next door have garden gnomes and two doors down rivals the Chelsea Flower Show, our front is paved. My parents are all for an easy life. Mum might as well have the mantra less gardening, more cooking. She's more yellow haldi fingers than green fingers.

Little sis is right. The only feasible way out of here is through marriage.

"Ello there, lovey," says Mrs Barker from across the street, as she tends to her marigolds. "Are you areet?"

I failed in my game of hide-and-don't-be-spotted.

"I'm good thanks. How are you?"

"Survarvin' love. Survarvin'. It's the old knees that are goin'."

"Well, it looks like you're fighting fit."

"Ah bless ya. You off out anywhere na-ice? That's a lovely outfit you got on there."

She can't be serious. "Oh this old thing? No it's my casual Sunday home wear. Thanks though but I'm just going to the shop."

"Well if that's ya home wear I'd love to see your fancy dress. You lot have the loveliest clothes. Them sarees are a dream."

I walk faster as I pass number 28, as I want to avoid any awkward cat-calling from Joe. He's the resident creepster and local handyman. He could really do with having an arranged marriage. Despite being in the same school year as big sis, he's never left the parental home. Worse still he's been chatting me up since I was 17. While some may be flattered to receive any male attention, I just cringe inwards, unsure of what to do. My usual resort is a nervous giggle. Thankfully, he's nowhere to be seen today.

As I approach the busy main road, a car slows towards me. I continue walking, picking up the pace. It's usually some loser trying to chat me up (I know that sounds arrogant but these gents are nothing to brag about), or someone about to hurl racial abuse. The latter is few and far between but I'm in no mood for either scenario.

"Oi oi! I thought I recognised you!" Calls a voice from behind the wheel.

Shitting hell! It's Peter from work. He pulls over at the bus stop. What's he doing here? Does he live here?

Before I could ask, he reads my mind: "I've just come from visiting me old mum. Do you live nearby?"

"Uh, Yeah. I'm on Willow Drive."

Why did I just say that? I might as well have invited him round for samosas.

"Some nice houses there. Not too cheap for a young lady. Do you still live with your parents?"

I note the emphasis on the word *still*. I suddenly feel embarrassed, like the 40-year-old virgin when his secret's out.

"Uh, yeah. I do."

"That must be nice. Mmmm... home cooked curry every day. I bet it beats those jars..."

Peter pauses, realising that his assumption is ever so slightly racist. But he's right on the money. Those jars are nothing on the real thing. He looks down at my outfit. I'm desperately thinking of an excuse to get away. A bus comes to my rescue, angrily beeping at Peter's silver BMW.

"Alright! Keep your err on! Anyway, I guess that's my cue to say goodbye. I'll see you at work on Monday. Oh and that's a lovely outfit by the way. Very pretty."

With that passing comment, which I couldn't differentiate from patronising or pervy (maybe it was both?), Peter sped away. And that is why I don't like to wear Asian clothes outside the house.

When I was younger, I so wished we'd lived in as Asian area. I was sick and tired of feeling left out and craved friends that I could truly bond with. Julia is brilliant. She goes above and beyond for me but she struggles to understand my world. The wonderful irony is that we all want what we don't have.

We used to make annual summer trips to London to see my uncle and second cousins. Mum was always eager to see her only UK based cousin and would pester big sis to book train tickets using our family railcard. Uncle Tariq lived in Tower Hamlets, East London, on the fifth floor of a tower block flat. They had next to no space. The lounge doubled up as a dining room, with an ornate, velvet upholstered six-seater table leaving precious little walking room. I remember squeezing past the table to get to the window, which was cranked wide open as the hot air created from layers of concrete flooring was stifling.

My uncle would smoke against the window ledge, wearing a lunghi and white vest and say to me: "Come look at the big city. Bright lights. This where you belong."

I would stick my head out of the window, breathing in second-hand smoke from my uncle and the Bengali neighbours puffing away on the balcony below. The polluted, humid air muffled the tobacco. I could hear a distant hum of police sirens. Canary Wharf would twinkle and the skyline was illuminated. It was muggy and smelly but I was enchanted. East London seemed alive, bustling, and bursting with Bangladeshis.

My fourteen-year-old cousin held a different view. "Man you're so lucky living in a white area," she said, loosening her floral scarf once we were in the privacy of her room. As she was the only girl, she had the good fortune of not having to share a bedroom, unlike her three brothers that had to make do with a metal triple bunk bed.

"Really? You can swap if you like? I'd much rather be here," I said.

"What, in Bangla-land, where everyone knows everyone's shit? Trust me, you wouldn't."

"But London has everything. Plus it must be nice to be among Bengalis and fit in, right?"

"Trust me, it's not. Sometimes it's better to be among whites, where no one cares for ya business. I can't even hang out with my boyfriend without being clocked."

"You've got a boyfriend?"

"Well yeah, why you surprised?"

"I just... I dunno."

"You mean you didn't think Bengali girls dated, innit?" She tutted and shook her head. "Bless ya... you really are a village bumpkin."

She wasn't done with the surprises though.

"Do you wanna see his pic?"

Before I could answer, she whipped out her phone to show me a grainy pic of a blonde haired boy with a buzz cut and green eyes.

"Proper fit, innit?"

"Erm, he's ok. Aren't you scared of getting caught though?"

"Yeah, that's why you can't tell anyone. I'm only sharing with you coz we're tight, innit. Anyway, it's only a bit of fun. We're all gonna marry freshies in the end."

"What's a freshie?" I asked. It wasn't a word in my twelve-year-old vocabulary.

"You know, fresh off the banana boat."

Still none the wiser.

"Oh come on! Fresh from Bangladesh. Like your brother-in-law. You know that's the route we're all going down. So you better have your fun too, while you got the chance."

As we grew older, we grew apart. Our family trips to London became less frequent. They eventually stopped.

I never once told anyone my cousin's secret. Then, just yesterday, I heard she's getting married.

"To an English boy," mum told me in hushed tones.

I'm not sure if said boy is the one in the photo, or another English boy. It struck me as odd how my cousin could live in the most densely Bangladeshi-populated area in the UK and still end up with a white guy.

"Is uncle angry?" I asked.

"Maybe upset inside. But he no show and telling me it's ok. *Boy will become Muslim*, he says. *And he give gold necklace, just like Bangla family*, he brag. I tell you, everyone think it's bad when someone else daughter do it. When it's in their house, they act all fine."

I wonder how fine mum would act if I did the same.

"But anyway, at least she getting married. And if boy convert, it's not so sharam," mum says without a second thought.

ON THE WAY BACK HOME from my milkmaid duties I decide that being on the phone is my best way of avoiding interactions with neighbours, or even work colleagues.

I try Julia. My call goes straight to her voicemail, which is recorded in her usual clipped, formal tone: *"Hi it's Julia here. Sorry I missed your call. Please leave a message with your name, number and a brief reason for your call and I'll return at my earliest convenience."*

*"Pleeeease come back to Manchester. I'm pissed off with everything right now. Otherwise call me. And you know who it is,"* was my thought-through reply.

I think there comes a point in every woman's life when it's time to leave home. If I was white I'd have permanently moved out by now. I got to go away for uni but the expectation was that I'd come back after graduation. I was happy to at the time. After years of living off Dolmio pasta, I was thankful to return to some home comforts. Yet sometimes I wonder whether I made the right decision. Or if I should have got a job in another city straight afterwards. Having been back for four years, I've become settled. Lazy. To move now seems a greater upheaval than when I left home with a large suitcase at the age of 18.

My phone pings with a message from Julia: *Can't talk now. On a lunch date with Vikram, the fit financier I told you about.*

*And it's going well (thumbs up sign). He's not an investment wanker at all. Call you later. X*

Without even trying, Julia has more brown boys to choose from than I do, despite me having a concerted matchmaking effort from an entire community.

I don't want to go home just yet, so I sit outside on our red brick garden wall and call Sophia.

She picks up. It seems misery loves company.

"Oh, I've had a bit of a crap day," she begins. "Just got back from lunch with the mother-in-law, which was hardly a pleasurable Sunday outing. She keeps badgering us about having kids. You know, she's like *oooh time is of the essence now you're over thirty*. Just because her daughter falls pregnant by sneezing... she doesn't get that it's not so easy for the rest of us. Why don't Pakistanis get that?? No tact. No shame. No *sharam*." She sighs. "Anyway, how are you?"

Sophia has just trumped my pity party.

"Well, I'm not sure if I should say. My problems seem so small in comparison..."

"Why what's up?" Sophia's keen to get to the point.

"Well, nothing really. It's just... it's just all a bit shit. Everything's getting on top of me. I'm tired of being at home. Every time I go upstairs I find my little sis. And it's really not her fault. I mean, where else should she go? If she had a social life I'd be jealous. And then I've been a bitch to mum and..."

"Hon," Sophia stops me in my tracks. "Do you think all this is getting you down for another reason? Are you just a bit cut up that it didn't work out with that rishtaa?"

I feel a lump form in my throat and my lip starts to quiver. I really don't want to cry.

"Probably. Oh it's pathetic. You must think I'm ridiculous. I only met him once. For two whole minutes!"

I'm embarrassed for myself.

"No, it's not pathetic or ridiculous. You basically met someone that you potentially thought you might marry. That's huge. And you didn't hear from him again. I'd be upset too. And it's natural that such a disappointment would magnify everything else. But the thing is," Sophia pauses thoughtfully, "younger siblings are annoying. Mums are annoying. But don't make them your punchbags. Instead, focus your energies on taking control. You wanna leave home? You wanna find someone? Then start looking. Make damn sure you've done everything you can to find a man that's right for you. Give yourself options. Then you won't get upset about one guy you met for two minutes."

Sophia's blunt and at times harsh but she makes a good point.

"I know, but it's so hard to meet someone. I didn't expect it to be like this. I'm about to turn 26 and I'm no further forward in finding a man."

"Don't take this the wrong way hon but you've hardly tried. Going to a couple of events isn't enough. You need to do everything you can to meet someone. I've always said, there are better girls out there than guys. In fact, the majority of Pakistanis are backward mummies boys and I'm sure it's the same for Bangladeshis. So it *is* hard. But you need to make it easier by leaving no stone unturned. If you just wait for your parents to find you someone... well, I hate to say it... but I worry you'll just end up marrying someone who ticks a few boxes."

"I know you're right, I'm just having a moment," I say.

"And you're allowed to have a moment. I know how crap it is when you're single and you feel like there's no one out there for you. But I promise you that there is. He might just be harder to find."

"I hope so. I just feel the pressure as it's the topic on everyone's lips. I've got my auntie coming over later. She's dad's youngest sister and she's well nosey. I know she's gonna grill me about what happened with the last rishtaa. I just can't face being around the questions... and the disappointment."

"Well you don't have to," Sophia declares. "Why don't you come to mine for dinner tonight? I'm making shepherd's pie."

"Oh, I don't want to be a bother," I say, though it's the best offer I've had in weeks.

"You wouldn't be. I always batch cook on a Sunday. It takes the pressure off having to cook in the week after work, so there'll be loads to go round. See how you feel and if you can sneak out for the evening, I'd love to have you over. And just remember hon – yes, I have my problems. But they're *my* problems. It doesn't mean they're any bigger than yours. So don't ever feel like you can't vent to me. I'll always have an ear for you. Plus we can talk about what we're gonna do for your birthday."

"Oh there's not much to celebrate there. Since moving back home, my birthday plans are decidedly low key."

"Well we'll do something low key together. And there is a lot to celebrate – we need to raise a toast to you finding a man. I think this will be your year."

Not many of my phone conversations are this cathartic. Just like Julia, I know Sophia's a keeper. In fact, I might even like Sophia more right now.

I've been out long enough. I head indoors and am hit by the smell of oil frying.

"Is Auntie coming now?" I ask, popping the milk in the fridge.

"Not yet. These for you. I thought they warm you and make better mood," mum smiles and hands me a bottle of tomato ketchup.

I take my plate of deliciousness into the living room to find my little sis, sans phone.

"Do you want one?"

"No I've already had some. They're all yours." She heads back upstairs.

I think that's our way of calling a truce.

I dunk the crispy corner of a samosa into the ketchup and take a bite. The savoury, spicy keema punctuated with sweet peas really does make me feel better. And one thing's for certain – I wouldn't get food like this anywhere but at home.

# 29<sup>th</sup> July, Going online

What happened with Tall-boy and his family will remain one of the great unsolved mysteries of our time. I've decided to go with mum's side of the story – that Auntie Fatima isn't returning our calls. Despite playing it cool initially, mum's now pretty pissed off about the whole thing, moaning about how annoying it is having a go-between as the chances of Chinese whispers are sky high.

I, however, have put Tall-boy to bed (not literally, that would be scandalous) and I'm moving on. After the horrible limbo of the last rishtaa, I decided that I need to take more control of my destiny. So along with my parents' matchmaking efforts, I'm upping my hunting game.

I turned one year older last week, so I'm officially on the wrong side of 25. I celebrated this milestone with a break from my usual Italian restaurant (Julia was in London that weekend) and instead I opted for a buffet meal with Sophia at the banqueting hall where we first met under the guise of raising money. It was much nicer going there without the pressure of hoping to meet someone. The food even tasted better. I'll take my parents and little sis next time.

In honour of my birthday, I did something I thought I'd never do... I joined a dating website. I've got Sophia to thank for taking the plunge. We've become fast friends. Older and more worldly, she's a great confidante, offering a fresh perspective as I navigate the choppy waters of this arranged marriage journey. She understands the Asian and Muslim side of things, while giving a more modern viewpoint than my sisters. She also has the patience of a saint, listening intently to my manhunt woes. Like Julia, she wants me to be more proactive and is constantly nagging me about going online. That's where she met Adnan, after divorcing her university sweetheart at 27.

"Look, I know you're not keen on the idea of joining a dating website. But it really isn't the last-resort, or embarrassing thing it used to be. Loads of people are on there, not just weirdos. And it worked for me, second time around," she reminds me with a chuckle as we sit with a plateful of starters at the buffet.

She scoops up some spicy chickpeas onto her fork and lifts it towards her mouth before putting it back down, uneaten, to continue her story. "I'm not gonna lie hon, my first marriage was based on looks and lust."

My face flushes a little. I've never heard a Muslim woman use the word lust.

"He was the kind of guy that everyone expected me to end up with. A gym bunny with a six-pack. We looked like the right fit. But it turns out that good looks alone won't sustain a marriage. Who knew?"

She still hasn't put the chickpeas in her mouth. I'm hungry and it's my birthday, so I continue crunching on my vegetable samosa.

Second time round Sophia was older, wiser and felt that the online dating world opened up a whole host of options for her. "Yes, there were a lot of dickheads. But there were also some really decent guys, from good backgrounds with good jobs. This time I knew better than to go for the meathead with nothing between his ears. I made a conscious effort to choose books over looks and it was the best decision ever."

Adnan's a doctor, though not the sexy kind you see on Grey's Anatomy. From what I've seen first hand, I would agree with Sophia. Those two are meant for each other. But I still had my reservations. I was careful how I relayed this to her, as I didn't want to offend but Internet dating felt so... illicit.

"I know there's nothing wrong with it. At least I don't think there is, as I'd be going online to find a husband. But still. Without anyone having done it before me, I just worry about how it will be received by my family."

"Then don't tell them," says Sophia, with a mischievous look in her eye.

"I guess... but you're gonna laugh when I say this. I've never done anything like this before and I just worry..."

"What EXACTLY are you worried about?" Sophia is as blunt as ever. She's still holding that fork with four precariously balanced chickpeas. She's about to put it in her mouth again.

"Just... I don't know whether I'll actually meet someone marriage material, or if I'll only meet knobheads that then recognise me at every family wedding for the rest of my life."

Sophia rests her uneaten chickpeas on her plate. I wish she'd put that damn fork in her mouth. She's making me look bad as I'm about to go for seconds. The chicken jalfrezi smells delicious.

"If they recognise you, you'll recognise them. So why should it be sooo shameful for you to be online, if they are too," Sophia reasoned.

This is where I realise the difference between Sophia and I. It's not just that she's older and has more life experience. Her family setup is different. Her folks are way more modern. Arranged marriages are all but obsolete in her community. All her older sisters, brothers and cousins met and dated their spouses before marriage. It was kind of expected she'd follow suit. Therefore online dating for her doesn't come with the same concerns as it does for me.

There's also another really stark difference between the two of us. During our early evening dinner, Sophia barely ate. She was so consumed with schooling me on online dating, that she hardly touched her meal. Nothing gets in the way of food and me. I did all the eating for her.

I ignored her suggestion initially. But after sleeping on it, I succumbed. Though I still feel like I'm doing something I shouldn't. This is a search for my future husband. If I meet someone online and it doesn't work out, I really hope they won't throw my Internet profile back in my face.

A few years ago, one of my second cousins got divorced. It was a BIG deal, made worse because they met through a marital advertisement in the Bengali newspaper. Of course, the real reasons for the demise of their marriage were likely to be complex. My cousin Akbar is a loafer who's never in work. His wife, from what I saw, seemed like she wanted more from life. She didn't want to be shacked up with her husband and in-laws who were around all day, every day. However, this was all brushed aside in the fallout.

My auntie simply said: "That's the problem with finding a bride in newspaper... you never know what you're getting. It's the last time we look there."

They then took Akbar to Bangladesh, where he married a girl that they hoped would better fit in with their standards and not complain too much.

With this very legitimate fear, I'm being covert about my online hunt. I waited until the coast was clear at home, which is rare. Coming back from work one day, I saw that there weren't any coats hanging in the hallway. I wasn't sure where everyone was but I didn't care. This was my chance.

I put myself on a Muslim-only dating site. Not to be racist and not to suggest that I'll only find Muslim boys on religiously specific websites. But time is of the essence and I can't be wading through a hundred Dave's and Peter's to get to one Javed.

Plus, there's one huge advantage with the Muslim dating sites – they're free for girls but boys have to pay a monthly subscription – Mmwahahahahahaha.

I'm guessing this is because more guys tend to go online than girls. It's terribly sexist and unfair for men but it works out quite well for me. Plus, given that the world usually favours the male species when it comes to gender pay gaps and life in general, I'm helping balance things out by making full use of my free subscription. You could say I'm a feminist pioneer in some ways.

Setting up a profile wasn't easy though. I mulled over a username. Some girls go for the cliché option of *Desigirl*, or even *Bengalibeauty* but I cringe at the idea of adopting a similar moniker. I just can't. Instead, I play upon my only discernible talent – writing. I type in *Wordsmith*. Damn! It's taken. I try *Wordsmith*1. That's available, so I snap it up.

The next part, filling out what I'm looking for, was straightforward enough. Male, Bengali, over 5ft 7in and living in the

North West of England (yes, you can be *that* specific). Then came the person spec. Even though I'm something of a professional wordsmith, writing about myself doesn't come naturally. I looked at other examples. Most girls write at length, detailing how friendly and down-to-earth they are, how they love family and cooking. They might as well throw in that they pray for world peace.

Some girls use religion to disguise their true intentions. For example, one girl wrote: *I want to find a life partner to explore this beautiful world Allah has created.* This roughly translates to: *I'd like to go on lots of holidays as I'm not allowed to travel before marriage.*

It all seems a bit corny. Those who know me will attest that I'm dry, self-deprecating and the opposite of whimsical. So writing a flowery profile goes against my very nature. Given the pretend modesty I had to convey during the rishtaa meeting, I'd like to be myself on this one. I keep it short and sweet. I say I work in PR, I'm family orientated and that anyone should get in touch if they want to find out more. It's possibly the shortest person specification in history. I'm hoping my uniquely elusive approach might create some intrigue at the very least.

Before uploading a photo, I check out the profiles of other girls for inspiration. There's a mixed bag of pictures. Some opt for traditional attire with photos taken at what looks like a wedding. Others have uploaded selfies that have been filtered to death. One girl even has a halo of butterflies around her heavily photoshopped face. Pity the guy who sees her in real life, expecting an ethereal bunny.

Foregoing the pictures we took in the park, I opt for a photo that's more me. I share a shot taken at my work's Christmas do, where I wore a long black dress, hair loose, and sparkly earrings. I won't edit the colour or enhance my features in any way, as this flies in the face of my core being. Plus, if I do end up meeting anyone in person, I don't want the boy to feel duped.

The site offers two options, have your photo made public for all and sundry to see, or have it on 'lockdown', so any interested boy would have to specifically request my permission to see my mugshot. It's a no-brainer that I'm going for the lockdown option. Why? Because apart from Sophia, nobody else knows I'm online. And I definitely don't want my family to find out.

None of my relatives have used dating sites (or at least none that I know of. They may also do it on the sly like me). Despite what Sophia says, I still think it comes with a stigma. Similar to the Western community, online dating is seen in one of two ways, either really progressive or really desperate. For Bengali people, it's often viewed as both. Putting yourself out there on the World Wide Web to meet and date perfect strangers is something that brown people struggle to accept. It seems a little fast and loose, a halal meat market if you will. This is hilarious in and of itself given the similarities between digital dating and arranged marriages. After all, just because we're conversing via the Internet, doesn't mean we'll be exchanging rude pictures. In fact, most girls seem to have the kind of respectable photos you'd expect to accompany biodata, even if some are heavily doctored.

There is, however, another reason for the online adversity from the community. It's the very real fear that anyone can pretend to be anyone from behind a computer screen. It's like the black market of dating. I've heard about people using fake profiles, fake photos and to make things harder, there's not a bio-data in sight to allow for the standard background checks.

HAVING HAD MY PROFILE up for a couple of weeks, I can understand why people have their concerns. No sooner had I hit publish, than my inbox was littered with half a dozen messages. Now this sounds exciting in theory and I was initially flattered. Boys have fancied me in the past, though none were marriage material. Usually they were the wrong race or religion. So having potentially marriage-appropriate Bengali boys take an interest (even if it was through a virtual forum) was exciting new territory. Despite vowing to be glass half empty, I couldn't help but feel optimistic that I'd avoid another rishtaa visit and find my own husband.

Then I started reading the messages. Allow me to divulge...

Boy no.1 – Opened his message with: *Hi, I've not come across you b4. Where's your pic? Got summit to hide?* He says this even though his own picture is on lockdown too.

I hit delete.

Boy no.2 – We exchanged a couple of fairly innocuous messages, before he said: *Oh you do boxersize, huh? That's good. I'm an amateur boxer. I like my women feisty as I love a good fight. We'll get on juuuust fine.* Does he mean shouty fighting or actual fisticuffs? Either way, I'm scared.

I hit delete.

Boy no.3 – In his profile picture he's wearing a turban and his name's Jasdeep. He's Sikh and obviously on the wrong dating site.

I hit delete. Sorry, I know that is totally racist of me but if anyone's surprised or offended by my actions, they haven't been paying attention.

Boy no.4 – He's just trying to flatter me by telling me what I want to hear. He claims to be so interested in PR and would love to know all about my career and hobbies. Nobody wants to know about my hobbies. I don't really have any.

But he's good looking, so I keep him on the back burner.

Boy no.5 – He's 5ft 3in. That's a whole two inches shorter than me.

I hit delete.

Boy no.6 – Starts with: *Salaam sister, how are you?*

Sister is a courteous and respectable way of addressing a girl you're not related to but in this context it just seems wrong. I look at his profile. He has a very long beard and seems very religious. He's not for me. So I politely reply to his message but don't solicit further contact.

Boy no.7 – He's not looking for marriage. He opens his message with: *Hey babe, how about we get off this site and you give me your number?*

I don't even have the words. I hit delete and block him from viewing my profile, which is a very handy function to have.

As I slam my laptop shut, my glass starts to empty. Is this the best the Internet has to offer? Online dating should have thrown up an entire world of new options. I was hoping to find some nice guys but instead I was greeted with a motley crew of flirts, misfits and plain-old oddballs.

*WHERE ARE ALL THE NORMAL GUYS?!*

After the initial anti-climax, my inbox continues to receive new messages each day. So there's quantity, even if the quality isn't forthcoming. I guess that serves me right for daring to dream. Why did I convince myself that I'd find the love of my life on the Web, anyway? After the build up of my rishtaa visit and the let-down by Heena and her possibly now-married pharmacist, I should know better than to count on anyone or anything.

I'm glad I didn't spend too long building my profile, if this is the standard of male talent. It's a good thing it doesn't cost me a penny, so it's not affecting my stingy ways.

# 26<sup>th</sup> August, No shorties or beard-ies

There are many similarities between the arranged marriage process and online dating, not least that both methods are unashamedly shallow. This is mainly because any element of chance is taken out of the equation. There's no random bumping into someone in Starbucks and getting to know them. You don't start out as friends before things naturally develop. It's straight down to business. You begin with the endgame in mind. Therefore, natural selection takes precedence – looks and credentials get you past the first round and into a meeting. In fact, Internet dating is even more superficial as there isn't a standardised biodata, so aesthetics come first. If your face doesn't fit, it's bye-bye.

I'm learning a lot about myself through this whole adventure. I'm figuring out what I'll settle for and, most importantly, what I won't. I used to see myself as a sensible girl that wouldn't choose a good-looking guy over a less attractive boy who's a keeper. Sophia always says that choosing looks over books never works out. When my first rishtaa's details came through, I made a point of reading his biodata before looking at his photo, even though mum went straight for his picture. The pervy cow.

However, now that potential candidates are coming in thick and fast through my inbox courtesy of my online profile and mum has signed me up with Mr Choudhury, a professional busybody, I've realised that I'm as shallow as the next girl. While I'm not expecting my future husband to be the brown Tom Hardy (though that would be bloody ah-mazing) there are limits to my level of compromise.

Mr Choudhury has sent us two candidates to consider. One guy is only 5ft 5in. I'm *nearly* 5ft 5in. Which means either a lifetime of flat shoes or rejecting this boy. I choose rejection and my mother, bless her, is 100% behind me. While she encourages me to keep an open mind during my quest to find a husband, when it comes to short boys that's a line we don't cross.

However, something mum and I can't quite agree on is how religious, or not, a boy should be. I pray (though not five times a day) and I keep all my fasts during Ramadan. I don't drink or eat pork (nor would I want to, the smell alone is enough for me to wretch). But I don't wear a hijab, nor do I attend any Islamic classes. This can make the search for a suitable spouse difficult.

One thing I noticed online is that boys fall into two distinct categories. Those that I'd class as very religious, they pray five times a day, have been to Hajj or intend to soon and sport a beard (in Bengali culture, this is rarely a fashion statement). They often prefer their future wife to wear a hijab. I'm just not that girl, at least not right now.

Then there is the polar opposite. The guy who doesn't pray at all, goes to bars, has had multiple girlfriends and probably drinks alcohol. He obviously won't want a girl who wears a hijab but I'm not her either.

And there's the rub. There seems to be very little middle ground. I've yet to find someone like me: not overly religious but not un-religious either.

The more I think about it, the more I realise that Tall-boy seemed smack-bang in the centre. The more boys I see and hear about, the more I realize he was quite a catch. It's a shame that ship has sailed (or to be more accurate, disappeared into the sea under mysterious circumstances).

Anyway, the other candidate's biodata suggests he is very religious. He has a beard (I'm not talking Gandalf but it's long). He's been to Hajj. It goes without saying that he'd want a wife who's just as practicing.

Mum's getting desperate, as she doesn't seem to see the problem. "So what if he be religious? That's good thing! You could learn some things maybe. Do you want to meet him? He might be nice."

He might well be lovely but if I don't turn up in a hijab, it's likely he won't want to see me again. And I'm not risking two failed rishtaas in a row. There's only so much rejection a girl can take. Plus mum's shifting attitude is laughable. She never preaches to me about being more religious. She watches Bollywood movies, for goodness' sake. When she said that my biodata would need to be adapted depending on the boy, I didn't quite realise to what extent.

The thing with religious boys is that I won't be pious enough for them. If I do decide to wear a hijab, I'll do it for me, not to please a potential spouse. Having differing views on religion can also present problems in the future. How will we raise our kids? Will he be happy with my chosen career, which involves the odd night out (though I generally loathe such socials and tend to nurse my glass of coke in the corner)? It feels like there are too many differences to make it work.

So, no beard-ies.

There is another condition in my fussy search for a man and it's super hypocritical. Centuries of colonialism have deemed dark skin to be unattractive and not just from the Caucasian perspective. Brownies don't like to be too brown. I'll let that irony settle for a minute. There's a reason that Fair and Lovely, a skin whitening cream, is a top-seller in South Asia. Fair is seen as beautiful and in this sexist society we live in, a pale complexion is even more important to men than it is to women.

It's something I've hated, as I've grown up on the receiving end of this discrimination. I'm used to the comments of "she's pretty, if not a little dark," or "you look really different to your sisters", and that isn't a reference to my big brown eyes.

One pretend auntie was even so blunt as to say: "How dis one get this much dark?"

Mum, who felt torn between maternal worry about my feelings being hurt and having to be polite to this silly old bat, turned her grimace into a laugh, responding with: "Oh what to do? She born this way." I was seven at the time.

I've often seen such digs directed at other people: "I can't believe he married her! They look odd as he's so fair. It's literally like day and night."

It's self-hating racism at its finest. And the worst bit of it all? I'm complicit. I don't know any other way. I apply a foundation that's a shade lighter than my natural skin tone. When choosing a new outfit, my first consideration is if the colour will make me look darker. I use sun cream from April onwards, even though the Manchester spring mostly offers rain.

It would be great to wear my dark skin like a badge of honour. Own it. But I can't. I don't know any other way. I'm no game-changer. I just want to be like everyone else. Not much has changed since I was a schoolgirl dodging questions about curry and family names. Whether I'm at home or out in the big wide world, I've always been a bit different and I'd really like, for once, to just fucking fit in. And if I can't, I'd like it to be easier for my kids. Of course, if I have dark-skinned children I'll still see them as beautiful and tell them so. I hope I can protect them from the shitty asides I grew up with. At the same time, I must think about the gene pool I'm creating. Let's face it, from colonial times to today, being brown is a hindrance in Asian culture. It might change a little with the next generation but I'm doubtful.

Tall-boy was quite dark, certainly more so than me. But everything else about him – his height, his family setup (did I mention his height?) was good, so it balanced things out. I guess if I were to use a pantone colour chart, his shade of brown would probably be the darkest I'd go. But my general rule is no fairer than me (I can't deal with the comparisons) but not *too much* darker either.

In the world of online dating I've seen all of the above – shorties, beardies and darkies in abundance. But on the plus side, it's helping me learn about myself – and I'm learning that I'm a superficial bitch.

# 7th September, Damned if you do, damned if you don't

Asian boys can be a funny, contradictory breed.

One particular online conversation brought this to my attention. A guy whose username was Badboy123 got in touch with me last week. I should have known better than to respond based on his choice of moniker alone. But hindsight is a wonderful thing.

His initial messages were friendly and respectful enough. You know, the usual stuff around hobbies, work and all that crap you spout before getting to the business end of the conversation, i.e. exchanging pictures or phone numbers. Though I hadn't seen what he looks like, his credentials stacked up. He's a 29-year-old architect from Warrington, which is half an hour from where I live. So far, so good.

He told me about a live chat function on the site that enables MSN-style conversations in real time. This, it turns out, is a mixed blessing. On one hand, it's good that we can have more of a 'conversation' – rather than sporadic messages – without having to exchange numbers. But the downside is that akin to a phone call, you can't think out your response.

And boy did he put me on the spot:

BadBoy123: *And a hello to you! How ya doin?*

Me: *I'm good thanks, how are you?*

Badboy123: *All good, I'm working on-site on a project today. We're building a care home in Salford.*

Me: *Cool, are you doing any of the building work, or don't architects get their hands dirty.*

Badboy123: Pfft. *Nah man, eff that. That's for my minions, innit?*

Me: *That's a nice way to talk about your team!*

Badboy: *I'm joking. They're sound but ultimately I make the decisions. They do the donkey work.*

I don't know what to say in response to that.

Badboy123: *Are you at work?*

I look around just to check nobody is hovering. Fiona's making another coffee and Peter has his head down at his desk, no doubt doing proper work. Luckily Maggie's out on a client meeting so my chances of being spotted skiving are slim.

Me: *Yes, though I'd use the term loosely as I'm clearly not working right now.*

Badboy123: *Hmmm... int-er-esting. So what are you doing later?*

Me: *Not sure yet, nothing planned.*

Badboy123: *Yeah, pull the other one. I bet you're meeting other lads off the internet, innit?*

Me: *Err... no.*

Badboy123: *But I bet you get lots of offers, innit?*

Again, not sure how to respond.

Badboy123: *So have you been in a relationship before?*

Woah! That knocked me sideways. I could see he was fishing but his segue was only marginally better than Fiona's non-existent one.

This is super dicey territory.

For the record, I have no boyfriend history to speak of. This comes as a surprise to many, given that I'm not in possession of three heads. Some people are even more surprised to hear this as I lived away from home during my university years. This is generally a rite-of-passage time when good girls cut loose and date anyone with a pulse.

However, while I had the odd admirer, I didn't dare date. Why? Because while most Bengali girls are God-fearing, I am very, very, very parent-fearing. Being the first girl to go away to university, I didn't want to do anything to let mum and dad down. At the same time, I wanted to fit in a *little*, so I chose my allies wisely. My friends were the girls who looked with their eyes (let's be honest – everybody looks) but didn't act on their impulses.

I was not expecting to be asked about this in such a forum. My first thought was to ignore Badboy123's question. I contemplated logging off and then getting back to him when I'd had the time to think of what to say. But that would look even iffier. So instead, I gave the worst possible answer.

Rather than a straight no, I say: *No, nothing serious.*

As soon as I hit send, I wish I hadn't. *Nothing serious?* I sound like a right floozy. It also doesn't help that I peppered in words like 'dirty' and 'loosely' in our last conversation. As Sophia says, it doesn't take much to get a man thinking all sorts.

I look at our chat screen. There's a pen icon next to his name, suggesting he's typing. Our conversation just gets awkward.

Badboy123: *Nothing serious? Mmm... In-ter-esting.*

Me: *No, sorry. I meant I haven't had a relationship before.*

Badboy123: *You serious?*

Me: *Yes. Why wouldn't I be?*

Badboy123: *I'm surprised. Why not?*

Me: *Erm, I just haven't. I guess I didn't want to mess around too much before marriage. Why are you so surprised?*

Badboy123: *So you messed around a bit (winky face icon)?*

He's trying to catch me out. What a shit. I don't reply. I'm not playing his games.

Badboy123: *It's just that most girls I know have been in relationships. Unless there's something wrong with them.*

Oh great, he's doing the opposite of slut-shaming... he's making me out to be a weirdo or prude and judging me for it.

Me: *Have you been in a relationship before?*

Badboy123: *Oh... fuck yes.*

Now there's really no need to swear at this point.

Me: *Have you had a few relationships?*

Badboy123: *Yeah, quite a few. I'm a bloke, innit. But I really respect the fact that you haven't. You just don't hear that with girls these days. Most of the girls I know have been around the block. Even with the ones I dated, I wasn't the first.*

What a hypocritical slag. On one hand, he wants a girl to be chaste and innocent like a precious flower. But as I've not dated anyone before, he thinks I'm a bit weird. Or he's peeved that I won't be easy.

This was one chat window I was happy to close down, so I made an excuse, saying I had to get back to work (which I totally did, I was meant to be writing a press statement for a client crisis) and we said our goodbyes.

I knew this guy was a total tool but I was intrigued to see what he looked like. You know, just to make sure he wasn't *so* good looking that I'd have to turn a blind eye to his blatant double standards. Since he's been so brazen with me, I decide to send him a cheeky request to see his photo. My chastity has left him enamoured. In less than ten seconds, he unlocks his photo. And who does this multi-girlfriend playboy look like? Enrique Iglesias?

Well, I couldn't say who he looks like but rest assured he's no Enrique. The dude's got no hair, a cone-shaped head and unfortunate neck rolls. It doesn't help that his photo is taken from a side profile, so the rings on the back of his head are piled up like a Michelin man. It resembles a corporate photo as he's wearing a dark blue suit and tie. No doubt one of his minions took it for him. The weird thing is, from the mid-shot photo, he doesn't look fat, he just has rolls in the worst possible place.

He swiftly sends a request for me to unlock my photo. Reciprocity would be polite. However, given that I'm not taking this any further, I don't really want this non-prospect to see what I look like. It's a small Bengali world, so the more people know I'm online, the greater the chance of my family finding out.

I decide to ignore his message. I know that's cruel but honestly, the fact that I even entertained someone who called themselves Badboy123 was a major lapse in judgement. Plus, given that I initially made the impression that I was a 'fun girl' who didn't have serious relationships, it's best if my cover isn't blown.

Note to self: be more selective when it comes to chatting in the future. And choose your bloody words wisely. You work in PR, after all. Words are your thing.

# 25<sup>th</sup> September, A date

Hold the front page – I went on a date. With a boy. And he's got me all confused.

He reached out to me online and his is one of the few messages that I haven't deleted. He's 5ft 6in (I know, I know. But beggars can't be choosers), lives in the next town from mine and has been to university. He also seems to be holding down a job in the local council. Nothing super-ambitious but again, beggars and all that. He's not the best-looking guy I've seen. He's got a very Bengali face (read: full rubber lips and big Bambi eyes). But that's OK, I don't want my man to be more attractive than me.

What's not so good is that he's the youngest of five. So he might be left with the parents when everyone buggers off. However, when he got in touch, I decide to get to know him with an open mind. We exchanged a few messages on email, mainly the biodata-esque stuff about where we're from, our families, etc.

Then, he plucked up the courage to ask for my number so he could text me. He was super-polite about it, saying that he totally understands if I'm not comfortable but he thinks it would be easier to keep in touch over the phone. I thought his old-fashioned chivalry was sweet. After all, swapping numbers is the natural next step and our email correspondence was sporadic as I only checked my messages at work.

After a few polite text exchanges, he asked if we could talk on the phone. I couldn't fault his game. He seemed decent, confident and forward enough to move things along. I silently applauded him. After all, isn't it the guy's job to do the chasing?

Speaking on the phone, it all started to go belly up. His confidence seemed to vanish. Our phonecall was practically one long silence from his end. Honestly, if I didn't ask any questions, I don't think he would have said a thing. I would transcribe it but it's just too awkward to put down in words.

I had to ask him how he was about three times, just to make conversation. He asked me the same, probably the same number of times. I'm not often lost for words but his socially awkward non-conversation rendered me speechless. I think I could even hear his brain ticking over, furiously thinking of a topic to discuss.

But here's the funniest bit. After we hung up, he sent me the following text message:

*Hey, I just wanted to say it was really, really good speaking to you just now. I know you might think we didn't speak much but it was enough for me to realise that you're a really, really nice person. So if you're comfortable, I'd love for us to meet up. But I totally understand if it's too soon and you'd rather speak more on the phone. Or not at all. Let me know either way what you'd like to do. Again, thanks for the call.*

Say what? Was he on the same call as me? I've had better conversations with the automated phone system at my bank. In fact, while we were not talking I managed to discover five countries I never even knew existed on my sister's giant world map on the wall.

Unsure as to what to do, I consult Sophia. Her response is predictably pragmatic: "The thing is, you're quite a chatty person. So maybe he regressed into being the quiet one and let you take the lead. Also, it's really hard to tell what someone's like over the phone. When I first spoke to Adnan, I thought he was cocky and smarmy. You know, typical arrogant doctor, thinking he's better than everyone else. It was only when I met him that I realised that he's just got a really sarcastic sense of humour. So I would meet this guy. You never know, he might surprise you in the flesh and come out of his shell."

Clearly the whole 'pack approval' mentality that exists in my culture is running through my veins, as I also consult my mum for her two pence worth. That might sound mad given my covert online hunting but one thing I've learnt over the last few months is that mum's actually quite modern and open minded about this whole marriage process. Yes, she might push the biodatas of beardies under my nose but it's not because she wants me to get married to someone very religious. She just wants me to get married, full stop.

Mum doesn't let on in front of dad – for fear of him accusing her of being a bad influence – but she has told me that she'd be happy if I met someone of my own accord. As long as he's Muslim and Bengali, of course. She might be modern by Bangladeshi-mum standards but not *that* modern. After the last rishtaa went tits up (though we still don't know how, why, or what happened), mum's become more open to the idea of my hunting efforts.

If mum were of my generation, she'd be a total minx. And for that, I have a renewed respect for her. Society, culture and shit-stirring aunties do their best to keep us girls in our place.

In spite of this, mum is doing what she can to make sure her daughters have more choices than she ever did.

Dad was the first rishtaa mum met and she'd only seen him twice before getting married. He ticked lots of biodata boxes – he was from a good family, he'd come to the UK to work in a restaurant in the late 60s and had gone back to Bangladesh to find a wife. My grandparents thought dad was a total catch. It was a no-brainer that mum would marry him. Luckily, dad is a sweetheart and has always been kind and gentle. In fact, I often feel sorry for him, as she seems to be the one that bosses *him* around.

Even so, she wanted more for us.

For example, when everyone else's daughters were getting married at 20, my eldest sister got a job and then got married at 23. While my older female cousins didn't pursue further education, my middle sister did a degree and masters. When everyone's daughters could go to their local university, I was allowed to study in a different city and live far away from home.

Now we're here, talking over a brew about this boy I met *'through a friend'* (telling her that I've met this boy online still feels like a bit of a stretch). Mum shares the same view as Sophia. She says there's no harm in meeting him for a coffee. I told you, she's a total minx.

It's nice to know that I've earned mum's trust enough for her to be comfortable with me meeting this boy by myself. I went away to university and didn't come back home with a boyfriend, or worse still, pregnant. She knows full well that I'm not about to tarnish my scandal-free record by engaging in what she would call 'funny business'. It also helps that I'm planning to meet him in broad daylight in a public place with lots of witnesses.

Having given the go-ahead, mum adds: "Good thing is, if he wimp, at least you get no trouble. You know it hard to meet good boy. So maybe if shy be his only bad thing, maybe it not so bad."

That's her polite way of saying don't be fussy. It makes me kind of sad to think that mum now believes my options are limited. I'm only 26 and most people say I could still pass for 20. But in Bengali terms, time is marching on. So someone I may have passed up on ordinarily, is now a serious prospect. I can't blame mum though, as I'm acutely aware that my male interactions thus far have been less than successful.

With my girl gang giving the green light and in the interests of seeing something through, I decide to give Shy-boy a chance. I'm keeping my fingers crossed that he'll have more conversation in person.

I ask him to meet me at a Caffe Nero on an industrial estate in Manchester, so I don't run the risk of bumping into any relatives – or Auntie Fatima – in town. She may be avoiding us but my rubbish pretend auntie has been spotted scouring the end of summer sales on the high street, so I steer well clear. Plus this estate is super easy for me to drive to and there won't be any issues finding a parking space. This greatly reduces the chance of me getting flustered en route.

One of the nice things about meeting a boy on my own terms, rather than as a formal rishtaa, is that I don't have to get dressed up like a Christmas tree.

I opt for a smart-casual look of jeans and one of my favourite pussy bow blouses with pink and white polka dots.

My outfit is still modest but much more me than my double deal salwar kameez options. I keep my makeup simple but do create a wing shape with my eyeliner, to highlight my best feature.

I arrive at the café to find it bustling, which is surprising given the dire location I chose. I'm assuming it's mostly people who work in the offices and factories nearby. He texts me to say he's upstairs, at a small table with dark wood chairs near the window at the back. Sensible choice. Opting for a rigid chair over the slouchy sofas adds the required formality for a first date. I don't want either of us to get too cosy.

It's nice that he's arrived ahead of me too. Maybe I was too judge-y about his possible shyness. I head upstairs and spot him straight away, as his is the only brown face there. He notices me as I walk towards him and springs up from his chair to greet me. He seems to get basic etiquette at the very least.

Neither of us know what to do next. He goes to shake my hand, quickly realises that's the wrong thing to do and then turns his hand up in a wave/ high five kind of thing. I mirror his gesture, though at this point I'm only about 10 inches away from him. We might as well have fist-bumped.

In the flesh, he's quite skinny and doesn't look much taller than me. However, his generously quiffed hairdo affords him an extra half-inch in height. I notice he hasn't taken off his coat yet. I wonder whether he thought I might not turn up?

As I take off mine, he says: "Ooh!" as though he's just made a big social faux pas. He hurriedly removes his blue quilted number, which looks like a high street version of a Barbour jacket, to reveal a maroon long-sleeved polo neck top.

I decide to initiate the conversation:

Me: "Have you been waiting long?"

Shy-boy: "No, just about 10 minutes."

Me: "Oh, that *is* long! I'm sorry! I'm not sure if that makes me very late or you very punctual."

He lets out a half-laugh, the one I use when I don't know what to say.

Shy-boy: "Do you want anything to drink?"

Me: "Erm, yeah. It's getting a bit chilly, so maybe a hot drink? What are you having?"

Shy-boy: "I think I'm gonna go for... a coffee. What can I get you?"

Me: "OK, you're gonna laugh. But I've never actually drank coffee in my life. I mean, I've tried it. But it's too bitter. Even the milkiest version. What is that? Cappuccino?"

Shy-boy: "I'm not sure. I only ever have regular coffee with milk."

Me: "Ah ok. So... anyway, I'm never really sure what to order when out for coffee. Not that I'm going on lots of coffee dates... Erm, but... I think I'll have a hot chocolate. And you thought you were meeting some sophisticated lady."

I laugh. He doesn't. God, how I wish I didn't always feel the need to fill the silence.

Shy-boy: "OK... so hot chocolate?"

Me: "Yes please."

Shy-boy heads downstairs to order. I think it's pretty obvious to all around – especially the baristas –that we're on a first date. A brown-person's first date, which is basically like a white person's date but with less eye contact, sitting further apart and certainly no hugging.

As he comes back, hands shaking under the weight of the tray holding two hot drinks, I notice how skinny his legs are. They're probably skinnier than mine, as his dark denims fail to add much volume. He's bought a packet of biscotti to go with our drinks, which is a nice touch.

He seems very thoughtful but is just as shy in person. Luckily we are sat in a bustling coffee shop, so the chatter of others manages to drown out some of the awkward pauses.

Me: "Thanks for my drink. How much do I owe you?"

Shy-boy raises his hands: "Oh no, it's on me."

Me: "Awww thank you. And thanks for meeting today."

Shy-boy: "No worries, thanks for coming too."

Me: "Did you have far to travel?"

Shy-boy: "No, it was just 15 minutes in the car."

At least he drives. That's one plus side.

There's a moment of silence. I'm not sure what to ask him next. I can see him scrambling for a subject. I dip my biscotti into my hot chocolate, thinking it's a cup of tea. I only realise my mistake when I take a bite and get a mouth full of frothy cream. Shy-boy doesn't notice my error but instead takes inspiration to dunk his biscotti into his coffee. He lets it linger too long and it dissolves into the hot bitter liquid. He huffs under his breath, like he's disappointed in himself. I pretend not to notice.

Me: "How's your work going?"

Shy-Boy: "It's OK, same old same old really. Um... yeah."

Me: "What is it you do again?"

Shy-Boy: "I work in IT. So it's a bit geeky. Fixing software issues."

He laughs. Hooray, he has a personality! And at least he's self-deprecating, like me.

Me: "I'm a geek too. I actually enjoy going into work. There's no bigger buzz than seeing my clients in the national press."

And back to tumbleweed. Neither of us speak for a painful few seconds.

Shy-Boy (finally): "What is it you do again? Journalism."

Me: "No, PR. Public relations. I pitch client stories to journalists."

He slaps his forehead. "Oh yes, of course. PR. Huh... sorry."

Shy-boy tightly wraps his thin fingers around his coffee mug, boney knuckles straining. Surely it's too hot to hold? I felt a bit bad for him, so I tried to chivvy along a conversation.

Me: "Oh don't worry. Nobody ever understands what I do. It's not as well known as the typical roles us Bengalis admire, like doctors and lawyers."

He doesn't say anything. I wish we were sat in a shielded-off booth rather than our very exposed table. People are starting to notice the tension. Over his shoulder I can see a couple who look to be in their early 20s. A real couple, wearing complementary grey hoodies and Adidas trainers. They keep glancing over at us and then smirking to each other.

Me: "But your work's going well?"

Shy-boy: "Yeah it's... it's all good. How about yours?"

Me: "Yeah, it's going good. One of my clients has renewed their retainer, so I'm hoping that's enough to get me a promotion..."

I stop myself from going into bragging work mode. Again.

Me: "So what are your plans this weekend?"

Shy-boy: "Nothing much. I think I'll take it easy."

I look out of the window, hoping to see something of note. Maybe a jumping off point for conversation. But alas, I've picked an industrial estate, so there's bugger all out there apart from anonymous looking storage containers and breeze-block buildings.

Our coffee date was like our phone call, only much more painful, as I could see as well as hear his shyness coming through. He looks like he's searching to say something else. I can't help but search his face too, to see if he's got anything to add. I'm out of ideas.

Shy-boy: "My nephews and nieces are normally over on the weekend, so I'll probably be chilling with them."

This pastime has come up more than once. I'm not against family, after all I have three nieces and two nephews myself and I absolutely adore them. But I don't want to spend every spare waking hour playing with small children. Shy-boy and I have been messaging each other two weekends in a row, not to mention the odd evening. And whenever I've asked him what he's up to, he said he's been chilling with his nephews and nieces. But here's the thing, you don't 'chill' with tiny people. You entertain them with toys and silly faces. This leads me to wonder whether Shy-boy has any friends.

Sophia, my twice-married mentor, always tells me to be wary of a guy who doesn't have friends. She says if he's a Billy no-mates, he's probably a bit weird.

Now, full disclaimer – my social life is hardly buzzing. Courtesy of having Bengali parents that have bestowed a vague curfew of 'come home before it's too dark' (which is a bitch in winter), my busiest weekends normally involve brunch, lunch or coffee with girlfriends. If it's a full moon, I get to have dinner and if I'm really lucky, I'll attend a thinly veiled marriage event, which annoyingly takes place in the evening. Even then, I'm the first to leave.

This comes across as rather odd to my more liberal Asian friends. Reena, my Gujarati girlfriend, would always think it's a bit lame that I could never stay the whole weekend when she hosts a university reunion. But I've said this before, Hindu Indians are perhaps the most modern species among us Asians. If you're a Bengali Muslim girl, weekend-long gatherings are not how we roll.

For Bengali boys it's different. They generally have much more freedom than us ladies, therefore have more of a social life. Yes, that's terribly sexist but it's just the way it is. This makes Shy-boy's lack of any activity beyond chilling with the kiddos a bit disconcerting.

The rest of our conversation isn't much of a conversation. I'm wondering whether he feels as awkward as I do. One thing is for sure – he is punishingly shy. Like wet lettuce shy. When he first messaged me, I was none the wiser. After all, anyone can be confident behind a computer screen. But in person? I'm just not so sure about him.

I mull over our coffee date on the way home. Does he have any friends? Does he have a social life? Is he from a strict family and not allowed to go out? Is he everyone's babysitter? But the biggest question of all is, can I get past his shyness?

On one hand, being a bit shy isn't a bad thing. I could tell from our conversation (well, my conversation mainly) that he would let any woman take the lead in life. So as mum says, he wouldn't give me any trouble. I know of marriages that haven't worked out because both parties are too headstrong. One of our pretend aunties got divorced at 35 after she'd had enough of her husband, who was basically an argumentative wanker. Sophia always says one of the main reasons her first marriage failed was because they were both stubborn (and he had a roving eye). So compared with that, shy isn't so bad.

On the other hand, if he's shy with me, does that mean he's going to be a wimp with everyone? Is he a pushover? Will his future wife be lumbered with the household duties because he won't speak up?

It's a tough call. I think of mum's words: "You know how hard it is to meet someone decent."

And she's right, finding Mr Right is hard.

Just as I pull up to our driveway, my phone pings. It's a text from Shy-boy. It reads: *Hey, thanks for meeting for coffee today. It was really nice seeing you in person and getting to know you a bit better. I really enjoyed our little chat too. I hope you have a safe journey home and enjoy the rest of your weekend. Look forward to seeing you soon.*

There are *sooooo* many flaws in his statement. We barely spoke. He didn't get to know me at all. Were we even on the same date?

I reiterate my feelings to mum when I get home, as she's eager to know how it went. Surprisingly, mum agrees that if he's a wet lettuce with me, he might be a pussy with everyone else too (obviously she doesn't say 'pussy', as she thinks that's a baby cat). I'm relieved to know that despite my earlier concerns that mum was getting desperate, she doesn't think I should settle for anyone. I'm told not to worry about it and that there's more fish in the sea. She also promises to chase our appointed busybody for more prospective suitors.

All that's left to do now is let Shy-boy down as gently as possible. I've never had to actually dump someone before (though we're not technically going out, it's still a rejection). I don't even know what I should say. I feel bad having to turn down a boy who is so nice and gentle. But a very small part of me is glad that it isn't me on the receiving end of a rebuttal. I just need to perfect my *it's not you, it's me* line.

# 3rd October, A common ground

The thing with shy people is, they're nothing if not agreeable. Despite my concerns about how to 'dump' Shy-boy, he totally understood. I wrote and rewrote my text message and ended up with some cobbled line about how I think he's a really decent person but we might not be the right fit for each other. And guess what? He flipping agreed with me! He thanked me for my honesty, said he understands where I'm coming from and that he felt the same, although he liked me and wished me luck in my search. It was a pain-free separation but I can't help but think that he would have agreed with whatever I'd said. *Meet up again? Sure! Get married tomorrow? What the hell, let's go for it!*

It's a relief to have avoided any awkward text exchanges with Shy-boy (I HATE confrontation) but I'm also pretty deflated. It would have been nice to at least have been pursued. Even just a little. It's also a pinch disheartening looking at the current spoils of my hunting. Thus far there's been a pharmacist that I didn't get to meet, a rishtaa that seems to have left me hanging and a bunch of online oddballs.

Middle sis keeps telling me you only need to meet that 'one guy', so it's natural to have some bumps in the road before then. But sometimes, I wonder if that guy even exists, as there seem to be more potholes than actual tarmac on this journey I'm on.

It's also pretty scary to see so many Bengali girls online that are over 30. Yes, I regularly check out the female profiles as well as the male. Partly I want to suss out the competition but I'm also terribly nosey and want to see if anyone I know is also using the website. The fact that women are getting older and remaining single could be due to a number of reasons. They're either shunning the dead cert of an arranged marriage and are solely on the hunt. Or they could be more focussed on their careers, hence marrying later. *Or* based on what my current efforts are suggesting – the pickings are slim. The latter worries me.

My email still pings, though not with the initial frequency but this is understandable. It's Ramadan, the holy month where we fast, focus on good deeds and abstain from any sinning. And while dating to get to know someone for the purposes of marriage is hardly a sin (I didn't so much as shake hands with Shy-boy) it just feels slightly wrong to hunt during this time. Plus, Ramadan bad breath is terrible, so the last thing you want to do is converse in close quarters with a prospective husband.

I also decide to use this time for contemplation, to clear my head and focus on the positive things in my life. One of which is my work. I've recently been promoted, so I'm now a senior PR executive. I also received a whopping 25% pay rise to boot. Maggie the legend decided to bump up my salary after her latest recruit – the one we all interviewed – handed in his notice. Whatever her motivations (most likely it's golden handcuffs), I'm flattered. I might be failing miserably in finding a spouse but I'm killing the PR game.

I'll probably stick with my current agency for another year or so and then look for something new. I've already scoped out the job market. All the good PR roles are in London. And truthfully, I would absolutely love to relocate to the capital. I often get to go there for work and I look in awe at the skyline, with its old architecture in sharp contrast with the skyscraper buildings. London is the land of diversity, opportunity and culture.

However, despite living away during my university years, I don't fancy relocating as a twenty-something singleton and doing the flat-sharing thing. I've also avoided guys online that are from London. Given that most suitors seem to still live with their parents, the last thing I want is to be shacked up with another family, while my own parents are over 200 miles away. After all, if shit hit the fan, where would I go? So I'm stuck for now, both in my work and personal life.

One of the nice things about taking a breather from hunting is that I've got more headspace to build relationships with my work colleagues outside of the office. I've started joining my team for drinks after work. This is something I used to avoid, because, when alcohol is involved, it's even more a case of the brown elephant in the room. Talk turns to favourite drinks (mine is Coke), how drunk they got on the weekend (never drank, can't relate) and their love lives (you know this bit).

I literally have nothing to bring to the table at these pub gatherings. However, mum encouraged me to suck it up and show my face for an hour, as there's a business benefit to mingling with colleagues. Though it's unorthodox for a Muslim mother to encourage her daughter to go to a pub, mum's thinking less about the location and more about the company.

"I read in Bangla peppar the other day to be good in business you need to go out with work peoples. It called network," she enlightens me.

Yet again, mum astounds me with her modern mindset. She was definitely born in the wrong decade. I've followed her advice and have been going along, sipping on a glass of coke and trying to find some common ground beyond work. But despite my best efforts, I usually draw a blank.

This week was even worse. As I was fasting, I didn't even put in my usual soft drink order. This didn't go unnoticed and predictably, the Ramadan questions came in thick and fast:

John: "Do you starve for a whole month?"

Rita: "Why do you do it?"

Maggie: "It sounds like hard work. It's not going to affect your productivity, is it?"

Peter: "Can you drink water? What? Not even water??"

I try to answer these questions as accurately as possible. And while I was expecting grumbles of how mad it is, Rita, who was intrigued as to the reasons behind fasting, simply says: "I think it's brilliant and it shows so much willpower. I went to Morocco during Ramadan one year. The locals offered us their food in the evening. Most people I know wouldn't want to share after not eating for a whole day. I've never seen such generosity."

To my surprise, nosey Fiona followed this up with: "My neighbours are Pakistani and every Ramadan they go round all the houses in our street offering the most amazing pakoras."

This lead to a conversation about deep fried Indian snacks. And for once, I was in my element. I can talk at length about food, especially spicy snacks.

"So what's the difference between a samosa and a shin-gar-rah?" asked Peter.

"Well, a samosa is the flattish pastry that you normally get in Indian restaurants. It's either filled with keema, sorry... mincemeat, or veg. Shingaras, as far as I know, are more of a Bengali thing. They're pyramid-shaped, with thicker pastry and filled with spicy potato. They're delicious but we don't have them often. In fact, I think the last time was in Bangladesh, when my aunt made them for breakfast."

Peter smiles and puffs his chest out like a proud peacock. "So that's what it is! Well, you'll be surprised to hear that I'm more Ban-glu-deshi than you. I had a shin-garrah the other weekend at my friend's wedding."

Peter has Bengali friends? I would never have guessed.

This seemed like a natural segue towards talk of arranged marriages but the intrusive questions never came. Instead, it felt like a balanced dialogue. Nobody was judging anyone. Throughout the conversation, I felt like my brown-ness wasn't an oddity. They were genuinely interested, there was no rhetoric.

After the first round of drinks, everyone started leaving. I was left with Fiona. The small square table we had congregated around suddenly felt terribly exposed. I looked around, the whole place had emptied.

Shit.

I couldn't leave straight away. It would seem rude. About five long seconds go by with no chat, while Fiona slowly sips on her wine, shooting wry smiles my way in-between. It feels like five minutes. I imagine how Shy-boy must have felt when he was desperately scrambling for something to say. I look at the food menu, it's nearly time to open my fast. I could use that as my reason to leave. But then I should at least make some small talk before I go.

"Can I get you another drink?" I ask, before noting that Fiona still has a full glass of red wine.

She raises it up, giving the wine a gentle swirl. "No, I'm good, thanks. Can I...?" Fiona pauses mid-sentence. She's already forgotten the whole I'm-not-drinking-or-eating-anything-as-it's-Ramadan conversation we just had.

"Ha! Silly me! You must think I'm a right ignorant cow," Fiona laughs, brushing her hand through her bobbed auburn hair.

I smile and say nothing. Then Fiona looks serious. "There's something that's been bothering me for a while... You've probably forgotten but yonks ago I asked you if you'd have an arranged marriage. It was only afterwards that I realised I might have put you on the spot in front of everyone... Oh! I knew you'd have forgotten by now but it played on my conscience a bit afterwards. So for what it's worth, sorry for being a nosey bugger. I'll mind my own business next time."

It's like she'd read my mind. I'm surprised she even remembered.

I feel emboldened. "Oh, I didn't even remember that. But thank you anyway. But if there is anything you want to know about arranged marriages, just ask me. In a more... private forum."

Damn, why did I say that?

Fiona looks relieved. "I'm so glad you're not offended. I was just intrigued as to how the whole thing works but I'm also glad that you won't have to go through it."

"Well Fiona... the thing is... arranged marriages have a bad rep but if you really understood how it worked, I reckon you wouldn't think it's that bad at all."

"Really?" Fiona puts down her glass and leans in, as if she's about to be let in on a top secret.

I get into PR mode, as I don't want to say the wrong thing. "Put it this way, if you were single –,"

"I am!" she interrupts with a gulping laugh.

"Oh... um... ok, sorry I didn't realise. I just heard you talk about your kids and..."

"I've got purl-enty of those! Three, in fact. It's the husband that's done one... You didn't know? It's the talk of the office... Behind my back, that is."

I didn't see that coming. This is what happens when you duck out of work socials, you miss all the gossip. I'm not sure what to say, except a pitiful sorry.

"It's ok. It's been a couple of years now, so I'm... get-ting there. Slowly. Still feels like shit though." Fiona reads my face like a book: "You want to know what happened, don't you?"

"Errrrm, only if you want to talk about it."

"Well then, better tell your parents you'll be home late. It's a looooong story..."

I open my fast with Fiona and a plate of fish and chips. We chat for what seems like an hour.

"So there you have it. Together for 18 years, lived with each other for 15 years, married for 12. And then one Christmas, just after we put the kids to bed, he says he can't do this any-more. Do fucking what??? Come home to a cooked dinner every night? Get to spend half an hour every evening with three washed, fed and watered children before I ferry them off to bed? Having to pay half the mortgage on a house that I NOW NEED TO COVER MYSELF?! Honestly, you think you know someone. You spend years, no... *decades*, getting to know someone. Trying to understand them. Keeping them happy. And then... nothing. It counts for nothing."

Fiona looks at me for a long time. "And the worst bit? He never told me why. No reason, no excuse. I don't know if it's a midlife crisis, another woman. I don't even know his living arrangement now. All I know is he's renting a flat which apparently leaves him *'no money at all'* to pay for his own kids. That's the most upsetting thing – they're his kids! The way he and the courts acted – makes it sound like all these years he was doing me a favour. Paying half for kids that weren't his own. Anyway... I'm rabbiting on. Weren't you going to tell me about arranged marriages? I might need one! I'm 41, I gave my best years to a bastard and now I'll never find a man."

I thought I had it bad.

As Fiona's been so upfront with me, I decide to be more honest about my man woes, which are admittedly insignificant in this context. I don't tell her all the ins and outs but I do say that our families introduce us to people, alongside our own hunting efforts. I also explain the logic of arranged marriages, and how the principle is to ensure that everyone has a chance to settle down and have a family.

"But look, I don't want to sound like I'm doing the PR for arranged marriages. I'm not. It definitely has its drawbacks. There is a risk as you have a short amount of time to get to know someone. But as you've shown... erm, anyway, regardless, it has its place. And I might have an arranged marriage, which I'm not upset about. I'd rather settle down than be..."

I stop myself. Clearly I've inherited a bit of mum's foot-in-mouth syndrome.

"On the shelf? Like me?" Fiona asks.

"No, that's not what I meant."

"It's true though. I am on the shelf. I'm the object of office pity, as everyone else over 35 is happily married. But even if you're not doing the PR for arranged marriages, I'm sold. It's a bloody great idea. I spent years living with a man and it didn't make our marriage stand the test of time. Who's to say that an arranged marriage would be any worse? If I'm honest...."

Fiona takes a big gulp of wine, before leaning in again. "... Bear in mind that this is my second glass of wine... but I think us white people need something like this. If we had the same idea, I wouldn't be on the shelf, at least not for the last FOUR YEARS! I'm a size-16, middle-aged with three kids. Where the *hell* am I gonna find someone? Nobody bothers to set me up, I can hardly go clubbing and I ain't doing no swipe-right crap. You... you and me... let's patent this idea now. Let's... let's go to the office tomorrow and when Maggie's not looking, we'll write a business plan – arranged marriages for white people."

I think that's the wine talking. She has to drive home, too. But drunk or not, the liberating feeling of being part of the conversation is making me share more than I ever would. I find myself telling Fiona about my online dating adventure. About the odd messages... about Shy-boy. It feels great.

My whole life, I've been left out of *that* conversation. In high school, when my best friends started to have boyfriends and swapped playing with dolls for parties and drinking in the park, they weren't my best friends anymore. I was never al-lowed to partake in such activities, and boyfriends were off-limits. Gradually, my friends and I had less and less in common and I found myself with a new set of friends, those who favoured books over boys. The only friend who stayed with me throughout was Julia, as she was more open-minded than most. She walked the line between hanging out with the cool kids after dark and doing lunch with me in the day. With the friends I'm still in touch with, our occasional meet-ups involve discussing work, as I sidestep any boy talk. Honestly, it sometimes feels as though we're more like acquaintances.

When I went away to university, I stayed away from the Asian girls who wanted to milk their freedom for all it's worth, throwing themselves at any Tom, Dick or Dawood. I put my allegiance with the sensible girls.

A lifetime in the cold made this honest discussion about the foibles of dating enlightening, for both of us. We didn't need to say it but, at that moment, we learned that we had more in common than we thought. It was also a reminder that everyone's got their own shit going on behind closed doors. This whole finding a husband business isn't just hard for me... it's hard for Fiona. It's probably hard for countless other women, too.

Fiona and I leave the pub around 8pm. She gives me a kiss on the cheek as we say our goodbyes. She reeks of booze but assures me that she's sober enough to drive home. Just as well, as we live on opposite ends of the city.

I've decided that I might just start being more open about my culture and background with my non-Asian friends and colleagues. After all, it sounds worse than it is by shirking the subject. Though I doubt I'll be shouting about it across a crowded office. I'm not quite that brave yet. Hopefully, now

Fiona's acknowledged her social faux pas, there should be less intrusive incidents.

# 29<sup>th</sup> October, An opportunist

One thing is for sure, the search for love (or at least a husband that we can grow to like) is nothing if not profitable. Fee-paying dating websites are in abundance for every race, religion and colour. Even every whim, as there's a site for married people looking for an affair. Though that's just being greedy.

Meanwhile, my mum is forking out on a monthly retainer to get the professional busybody to send biodatas through our letterbox. It seems that nobody wants to set anybody up out of the goodness of their own hearts. Everyone is cashing in on other people's... well... desperation.

They say you can't put a price on love but I wish this manhunt wasn't so costly. We need some spare change for the wedding. Therefore, it's a relief – and surprise – when Julia comes good on her mission to find me a man.

We met up with our mutual friend Helen for lunch at our Italian the other day. She was one of the bookish girls in school and hasn't changed much a decade later, though she's developed a love for the great outdoors of late. I've barely sat down and I'm ambushed about a weekend away she's organising.

"You haven't got back to me yet about glamping. Do you want to come? Joy and Claire have already confirmed."

"Erm... I haven't checked my diary yet," I lie. I know full well that I have nothing going on but the thought of being shacked up for a weekend with three other girls while they get progressively more drunk and angry about men fills me with dread. It's not the bitterness towards men bit that bothers me, as I'll be in good company. It's the boozing. Helen's a crying drunk. She bawls every time she's smashed. They're full on, angry-at-life tears. Her glasses steam up and everything.

"Oh, we've got that thing, remember? You were going to stay with me in London that weekend... you know... to hold my hand during speed dating," Julia lies for me.

She's the best and she also has no intention of spending the weekend comforting a crying Helen.

"Gosh, you two! Boy mad!" Helen scoffs.

Julia disguises our collective relief at getting out of glamping with a giggle. "You don't know the half of it!"

As we're chatting over olives and bruschetta, Julia shares her latest dating disaster. She met a guy while on a photography expedition in Shoreditch. The excursion was organised through meetup.com, a website where you can find events run by like-minded people and there is something for every hobby. Since moving to London, she has joined the East London Art Lovers group, the Alternative Cinema club and even attended a chess tournament. In all the years I've known Julia she has never expressed an interest in photography, foreign-language movies or chess. Basically, these groups are the mainstream equivalent of thinly veiled marriage events. Over 90% of attendees are single and more than ready to mingle.

"He seemed normal enough during the photo meetup," Julia begins. "So we agreed to go for dinner afterwards, and this is where it all went downhill."

I brace myself for what horrendous cardinal sin this boy could have committed. Maybe he didn't open the door for her? Or perhaps he failed to kiss her hand as he ushered her into his chauffer driven car? It's not that I'm saying Julia is fussy but she was born in the wrong century. She longs for old-fashioned chivalry, the Gone with the Wind romance that hasn't existed for about 100 years.

"Anyway," she continues, "when it came to paying for the bill, he started pulling out all these *pennies* from his coin purse. And yes, he had a purse!"

Oh, dear. Julia's always drawn the line at boys who don't pick up the tab but I never knew she had an opinion on the number of coins required to make up the tab.

"He was counting each coin *painnn*-fully slowly. Even the waiter was mortified for me. After that, I just couldn't date him again, so I didn't return his call," Julia concludes. Then she turns her attention to me. "So that's my latest boy update. What's new with you?"

Now, I try to steer clear of arranged marriage conversations with anyone other than Julia but I decide to share details of my date with Shy-boy. After all, I had a date. This was newsworthy in itself. When I tell the girls how it didn't work out and I'm feeling time-pressed to find a man, Helen throws in a pearl of wisdom.

"You can't rush love," she says.

I reckon she got that line from a movie, as she has no love life to speak of. After college, Helen studied at our local university and now works for the local council. She's never had a boyfriend. She's rocked the same full-fringed shoulder-length haircut since school, though she did once experiment with dyeing her ginger hair brown. Helen still lives at home with her parents (yes, I know I do too. But I'm Bengali, so it's different) and has a cat called Jumbo. But more to the point, SHE'S NEVER HAD A BOYFRIEND. And she's nearly 27. On paper, Helen is more Bengali than I am. She is totally going in the direction of my sister's friend Laura, who is eternally single. I don't want to be like Helen or Laura, so I'm adding a little urgency to my quest for love.

Helen leaves our lunch early, as she's got book club afterwards. So Julia and I are left to share a profiterole dessert. I miss these catch ups, they're becoming a rarity as Julia gets more settled into her life in London. I'm keen to find out how she's getting on, diabolical dates aside. Then I realise the time myself. I was meant to pick up my little sister from badminton 20 minutes ago.

I hastily say goodbye, leaving more than enough money to settle my share of the bill, before Julia stops me in my tracks with a big surprise: "I was waiting for Helen to go as I wanted to tell you, I might have found someone for you!"

Her news comes at a good time. Ramadan has ended, we've celebrated Eid and I'm out of my self-imposed boy ban and back on the hunt. As I have to run, I promise to call Julia as soon as I've picked up the brat.

Once my carpool duty is done, I look around my house for some privacy to make a call. My teenage sister runs upstairs to hole herself up in our bedroom. She hasn't even bothered to shower after her class. Mum's just come in from the garden after hanging out the washing. She heads straight to the kitchen to attack the grey and yellow diamond-printed lino with a mop.

Dad's in the living room, watching the news on the Bengali channel.

I enrobe myself in mum's lilac paisley-print pashmina and retreat to the garden, as I can't wait to hear what Julia has to say. No sooner does our conversation start, than dad comes into the garden to check on the clothes mum has just hung out. They're clearly not gonna dry that quickly.

He spots me and says: "Eh-he, you on phone?"

"Yes dad."

"Ok, ok. You talk."

Usually people say this when they leave you to it. Not my dad. He continues checking the clothes – which are still dripping wet – before looking at the autumn-ravaged raspberry bushes. It's not that dad's one of those super-strict parents that will scold their daughter at any whiff of boy talk. He's just inherently nosey.

I let Julia do the talking and respond with "mm-hmms," and "oh ok's," so dad can't figure out the gist of the conversation.

Julia realises from my responses that I need to be discreet and says to me: "Just to be on the safe side, I'll use the letter B instead of boy."

She really is a sister from another Mister. But she begins to speak in riddles, which only confuses things. I manage to deduce that Julia doesn't know someone specifically, she knows someone who might know someone. In fact, as if it wasn't convoluted enough, she knows this acquaintance through another friend. It's like the seven-degrees of rishtaas.

Apparently, this friend knows a couple of guys. While I like to think I'm modern minded, dating two guys at the same time is a bit much for me. But I'm keen to find out more from this friend of a friend of a friend. Julia's vague about the details, as she doesn't know much herself. What she can tell me is that this girl, Zahra, is Bengali, a bit older than us and seems to be well connected. I take her number, and after a text exchange with Zahra, I agree to call her on Monday on my lunch break.

This is where it gets interesting.

I call Zahra from my car and quickly realise that it's a good thing I ring-fenced an hour for our call. This girl can *talk*. Mainly about herself.

The first 15 minutes of our chat is all about Zahra blowing her own trumpet: "So I'm an accountant by trade but that's really just a small part of my life. I'm really, really heavily involved in the community. All in my own time, at my own expense. I've always been passionate about working with people. Our people. Our Bangladeshi women and the next generation, just to ensure they have the best opportunities. The kind of thing you and I take for granted."

I want to joke that it sounds like *she's* the one looking to get married the way she's PR-ing herself, not the boys. But I don't have the balls to be so bold. I continue to listen, though I'm getting bored.

"Umm... let's see what else. I've hosted lots of charity events. I *think* the last one raised £5,000. No, sorry, that's £6k, for an eye hospital in Bangladesh. Through doing this I've become really well known in the Bangladeshi community. Without even trying really. Even people from different castes and backgrounds know my name, people I'd never really interact with otherwise. Anyway, um... what else... what else. To be honest, I could go on forever but you'd be better off Googling me. Everything should be on there."

She's beginning to sound like a real wanker. Zahra continues harping on about her life, while I'm eager for her to cut the crap and get to the good stuff.

Finally, she talks about the boys. The first boy, she says, is from a very respectable family, originally from Dhaka, the capital of Bangladesh. I'm from Sylhet, a smaller town. Historically, those from Dhaka turn their noses up at us Sylhetis. It's kind of like the north vs. south divide in the UK.

I continue to listen. His dad apparently works in Washington and his mum is a retired teacher. That trumps me. I'm the daughter of a retired restaurant owner and housewife. Based on biodata-type stuff, this doesn't sound like a match. But I listen on, hoping this boy might potentially overlook my parents' lack of career credentials and be impressed enough by my PR job.

Without taking a breath, she moves onto boy no. 2. According to Zahra, he's also very impressive, as he works in investment banking in London. She fails to mention how she knows these guys. Apparently, she's collected the details of dozens of eligible bachelors, becoming something of a matchmaker in the process. I joke that she should keep a spreadsheet. She laughs and tells me she's got one.

I smell a rat. An expensive rat.

Zahra continues: "So I can get you in touch with these guys, if you'd be interested?"

Mug that I am, I say: "Erm... potentially."

But then comes the money shot, quite literally.

Zahra says: "But the thing is, this all takes rather a lot of my time. I make sure I see everyone face-to-face and vet them beforehand, to ensure that they're good decent people. I do all the background checks, which is the really important bit. As a woman, a *Muslim* woman, you want to feel safe when you meet a guy for the first time. So I take away any worries. And like I said, I've got loads of guys like this on my spreadsheet."

She clears her throat: "So the way I do things is... I basically charge an annual fee of £500. For this, I will arrange a minimum of six introductions for you. I won't set you up with just *anyone*. If I don't see you as the right fit for a guy, I won't put you in touch with him. So what do you think?"

I can't believe it. She's another fucking busybody. But worse, she disguises her services as if she's helping a sister out. She's dangled two boys in my face but is holding them ransom for a princely sum. And to top it all off, she throws in the religion card during her business pitch.

I have so many follow-up questions as her services made no sense to me. If she's already met and vetted these two guys on her spreadsheet, am I paying to have myself vetted? What if the first introduction turns into my dream man, do I get part of my fee back as she's promised five more introductions? Or do I just go along to these dates to get my money's worth? And most importantly, who the hell is *she* to determine who'd be the right fit for me?

Suddenly, I grow a pair of balls. I don't know if it's the pent-up frustration of my whole fruitless search, or the sheer anger at Zahra's bullshit but I let rip.

"Are you having a laugh?" I belt out. "My friend Julia genuinely thought you were going to introduce me to someone out of the goodness of your own heart. But clearly everyone has a price. If you were selling a service, you could have just been up-front and said that, instead of chewing my ear for half an hour telling me about how brilliant you are."

I hear Zahra trying to interject but I'm on a roll and this train of anger can't be stopped. "That's half an hour of listening to your bullshit that I'll never get back. And now I'll never get to Tesco in time to get my meal deal. So thanks a bunch. But also, no thanks. Find yourself another mug."

Before Zahra has a chance to respond to my rant-y mono-logue, I hang up. My fingers are trembling. Did I just say that?? I'm shocked at myself. Whenever I've felt wronged, I've not spoken my mind. Society – be that British or British-Asian – encourages a stiff upper lip. I even chose a career in public re-lations, which is all about saying what people want to hear, rather than what we truly think. My work is based on being liked rather than being right, or even honest. And that's how I've been most of my life.

I couldn't call out Heena for teasing me about the phar-macist, for fear of sounding desperate. I stopped chasing mum about Tall-boy, for fear of sounding desperate. I constantly dodged the subject of arranged marriages at work, for fear of being singled out as the strange brown girl in the office. But every woman has her breaking point. For me, someone who purports to help me out while actually pedalling their services and cashing in on sisterhood is a step too far.

On reflection, I might have been a tad aggressive but I'm not sorry. Once I explain Zahra's true intentions to Julia, she'll understand why I flew off the handle.

I'm exhilarated. Hungry but exhilarated. I found my voice when politeness would often be my tone of choice. As I make my way back to work, I'm hoping that nobody ambushes me with an ignorant question about arranged marriages, Ramadan or just being brown in general. Today is not the day.

As I enter the kitchen and try to fashion a lunch from the fruit porridge I forgot to eat yesterday, in walks Carol, the office secretary.

Seeing my porridge, she exclaims: "Oh I didn't think you'd be eating this month. Should I call the Ramadan police?"

Oh well. You can't win them all.

# 30<sup>th</sup> November, A tale of two rishtaas

Well, it's been a busy month.

It seems that my newfound assertiveness has rubbed off on mum, as she rang Mr Choudhury, our professional busybody, to give him a right good bollocking about the lack of talent he's sent our way. When I say bollocking, I mean in the Bengali way. She's still polite, voices aren't raised and the conversation starts and ends with a salaam. But she gets her point across.

Mr Choudhury shares his sincerest apologies and explains how busy he's been at work (his real office work), which is why he hasn't had much time to send over any suitor details. He also mentions in passing something about his uncle in Bangladesh being unwell. Call me a bitch but what's that got to do with anything? I suspect he's thrown in an extra fib to cover up his half-arsed-ness. In fear of losing his monthly subscription, Mr Choudhury pulls his finger out and sends three biodatas in one big brown envelope the very same week.

My heart sinks a little when I see the first photo. He's actually Boy no.4 that I met online. The guy who was basically telling me everything that I wanted to hear. He went quiet for a while on the messaging front, which I suspect was down to him chatting to someone else. I'm not one to judge, as soon afterwards I started speaking to Shy-boy.

Then he got back in touch before Eid. His message was unexpected, not least because we were still in Ramadan and my online activity had died down but I assumed he wanted to get a head start on the other boys on the site. He apologised for being elusive and explained how he's been super busy with work. It's likely that he was lying but didn't want to be so brazen as to say he was speaking to another girl. I also colluded in the lies with a tall tale about how I've been busy too, and that I'd recently been promoted. That bit was true but I failed to mention that I met someone else in the interim.

The funny thing with this process is that despite the fact that we're all actively looking, chatting, meeting... nobody talks about it as it feels like we're cheating on someone we're not even dating. It's bizarre but I go along with it, anyway.

I failed to document this dalliance, as my conversation with Boy no.4 ended just as quickly the second time around as it had begun. This was because... it pains me to say it... he didn't fancy me.

After a few quick messages, he asked if he could see my picture. It was fair enough as I'd already seen his photo which was made public from the outset. Plus I didn't want to have an endless conversation with someone who hasn't seen me. After Shyboy, I didn't want to drag things out with someone who wasn't the right fit.

Now Boy no.4 is pretty damn good-looking, with fair skin, a chiselled jaw and sharp features. The kind of guy that would get noticed at a thinly veiled marriage event. Deep down, I knew he might be too attractive. He went against my criteria by being prettier than me. However, out of politeness, obligation and a bit of hopeful optimism (I know, I know), I unlocked my photo. And you know what? The cheeky bastard went quiet. Again. He didn't even acknowledge my picture. He didn't even respond with some innocent message and let our conversation fizzle out naturally. He didn't even say thanks but no thanks. He... just disappeared.

Natural selection is a bitch. And so is Boy no.4.

I can't cry foul play as I've done my share of superficial rejecting. Mum is often moaning that I'm never going to get married if I keep turning down the rishtaas that come through from Mr Choudhury. To be fair though, the last photo he sent was the brown incarnation of Quasimodo, hence the angry call from mum demanding a better calibre of men. But the way Boy no.4 just fell silent really stinks.

You can imagine my dismay when I see his smarmy face staring back at me in full, printed glory. Mum still doesn't know I'm online and I'm hoping that she never will. Now the two realms have collided and come full circle. The arranged marriage world and the online dating universe have been bridged by bastard Boy no.4.

This presents a real dilemma. I clearly don't want to meet this boy but how do I outright reject him without making mum suspicious? After all, he's the best-looking rishtaa photo to come thus far. More handsome than Tall-boy, who mum knows I was slightly gutted about. I can't even poke holes in his biodata. He's geographically appropriate, has a degree and works as a dentist. Mum and I both have a soft spot for anyone working in the fields of medicine or finance.

I say that I don't want to meet this boy. Mum naturally asks why, so I tell a half-fib. I explain that a friend had actually suggested him for me but after exchanging photos, he wasn't keen.

It hurts my ego to tell mum that he didn't like me. I think it upsets mum too, as she's as Bollywood as I am, and would love for me to end up with a hottie. But she understands that we need to let this one go.

A real saving grace of the archaic, formulaic biodata tradition is that the boy's family normally send their photo over first, giving the girl's side the option to refuse without exchanging pictures. So Boy no.4 hasn't received my details and can't reject me twice. Nor can he tell anyone we met on the Internet. As he lives about 25 minutes from me and the Bengali community in the north of England is small, news of my online presence could spread like wildfire. So on this occasion, thank fuck for outdated, slightly sexist rules.

The other two biodatas are more promising. First, I haven't spoken to either on the Web. Second, neither is ugly, though they couldn't be more different.

The first boy looks like the opposite of a beardie. In his photo, he's pictured in front of a bar, wearing a black fedora hat. It must be a fancy dress party and I'm hoping he was only on mocktails. His black shirt is unbuttoned slightly beyond what is considered decent. He's of a similar complexion to me and he might be bald, or at least have a shaved head. I can't quite tell because of his stupid hat. His face isn't one I can pick fault with. He just looks... normal, I guess. He's got a slightly big, bulbous nose but then so have I. On a good note, he's a pharmacist and has a muscular build, so I decide he's worth meeting.

The second boy's photo seems to adhere better to the arranged marriage guidelines. It's a standard mid-shot photo of him sat on a sofa at what looks like the lounge of Nawaab restaurant or some other fancy banqueting suite. He's wearing a navy suit and tie and looks slim, borderline skinny. He's got an unquestionably full head of hair, is fair skinned and smiley. He's got thin lips and smallish, deep-set hazel eyes. However, he's only 5ft 6in, barely making the height grade by a whisker.

Mum and I are also unsure of his work. His biodata simply states that he's in management. But Bengali people are notorious for exaggerating their job roles – a teaching assistant is always referred to as a teacher, a paralegal is always a lawyer. We decide that we'd need to quiz his occupation if we decide to meet.

As I haven't said an outright no to either rishtaa, mum shares both photos with dad and little sis.

This time around, dad shows a tiny bit more interest. He takes one look at each photo, coughs a little, before asking: "Ok... ok... which village in Bangladesh is he from?"

Satisfied with both boys' respective motherlands, he then passes the photos back to mum and gives his usual verdict: "Yes, yes. That's fine. If you think they're OK. Maybe one with the hat be bald. But otherwise OK."

That's about as involved as dad will ever get. I do love his hands-off attitude. Unlike some families where the father rules with an iron fist, my dad happily lets mum take the lead in what he thinks is 'women's business'. But he still has an opinion on the looks of his prospective son-in-law.

My little sister finds the whole thing hilarious. I see her assuming the role I occupied when my middle sister was getting married. She's the comedienne, making a mockery of Fedora hat-boy. She looks at the other photo and says: "He's a short-ass. I bet he's smaller than you."

I'm not offended. Her opinion doesn't really count.

With both boys being potential contenders, mum does something completely unorthodox. She requests meetings with both suitors and their respective families on two consecutive weekends. Traditionally, you see one boy first and if that doesn't work out, you then arrange to meet the other boy's family. This long standing, unwritten rule has been passed down to me and is something I exercise outside of the arranged marriage process. I've only been talking to one boy at a time online. However, mum was throwing the unwritten rulebook out of the window.

She calls Mr Choudhury with her request and I can hear through the phone that he is unsurprisingly aghast. But then mum simply says: "I don't see what problem is? All boys families do same thing. We got two photos, why not see double boys? More choice, better choice. Just like job interview. Need to try lots for best job. This same thing."

It seems like mum is growing fatigued by the long, polite arranged marriage etiquette and becoming all too aware that other families frequently flout this exclusivity rule. So she's bending the rules herself. And for this, I applaud her. She's turning into a trailblazer among Bengali mums. Sensing that he might lose his £30-a-month fee, Mr Choudhury reluctantly agrees to mum's request.

I told you it was a busy month.

Mum is surprisingly relaxed about these rishtaa visits. There's none of the ceremony we experienced the first time round. My older sisters are invited but only middle sis could make it. Big sis promised to attend the next weekend, like there's some kind of sisterly rota.

There's no shopping for new outfits, as I've still got an unworn salwar kameez from my double deal. Plus the first one's only been worn once. And it's highly unlikely that my rishtaas past and present are all going to get together and discuss my sartorial choices. I'm seriously hoping they don't all know each other.

But one thing mum does is prepare an abundance of samosas. She is nothing if not a feeder. I catch her folding vigorously the day before the first rishtaa visit. I'm about to head out to the shops but I notice she looks tired. I sit down to help.

"Mum, why do you have to go to so much effort? We could have just bought some samosas from the Asian shops. Some brands are pretty authentic, just like home cooking."

Mum looks as though I've sworn at her. "Dooro!" This roughly translates to *Oi, that's out of order*. "And have people say bad about our food? Everyone already talking so we don't need any more –," mum pauses.

People must be talking about me and my single status.

"Anyway, no. I make with hand." She returns to her folding.

I tentatively spoon some keema onto one end of a strip of pastry and start folding.

"But it's such hard work for you. Maybe instead of samosas we could try something different. We could make kebabs. They just need to go in the oven. And we could buy a bunch of cupcakes. From the patisserie, not the supermarket. They'd love it so much they wouldn't care if they're shop bought."

"I told you, home food! When you have daughters to get married, you buy cakes! You no have to cook smelly food. Be as English as want!"

"Mum, I didn't say anything about wanting to be English. I love our food. It's not smelly."

"Not what you say before. I stopped eating shutki for you."

"What? I never said don't eat shutki. I hated the smell but –,"

"Yes, so I stopped. All things I do for you girls. Even don't eating my favourite food so kids no embarrass."

Mum blinks her eyes for a long second, like she's holding back tears, before grabbing a spoonful of keema. Her samosas are perfect acute triangles. I look down at mine. It's an isosceles and a wonky one at that. I've also overfilled my pastry, the oil is leaking out of the corner.

"How come yours are perfect, and mine are like this?" I ask.

"Look, I show you how," mum replies, demonstrating her well-honed folding technique. She creates a triangle, slowly, delicately, before adding in the keema. I was all gung-ho and just plonked on the mincemeat, forcing the pastry around it.

She's made about 80 so far, all neatly lined up on a silver tray. Each one takes time and patience to make but is eaten in seconds. I bet she's lost count of the number of times she's covered this table with a clear plastic cloth and sat folding dozens of samosas, despite never getting round to eating any herself. I shouldn't take for granted how much mum does for us. From making samosas by the truckload for boys I may not marry, to not eating her favourite food for years as we're embarrassed by the smell.

I remember the stench of shutki wafting from round the corner on the walk home from school. During my first year of high school, a bunch of us would journey back together, even though we weren't necessarily friends. This eclectic group included Carly. It was unfortunate that mine was the first house everyone would pass before cutting through the country park to get to their respective homes.

Carly once said: "Eww, what's that?" Before realising, to my mortification and her amusement, that it's coming from my house.

This led to a chorus of subtle sniggers and a helpful comment of: "Ooh, I think your dinner's ready!"

Julia was the only one who pretended not to notice.

To make matters worse, as we approached my house, I saw mum putting the bins out. That was the last thing I needed. As if the shutki stink wasn't enough, my saree-clad mum was about to throw herself into the ethnic mix. I might as well have had a sign on my back, saying *kick me, I'm different*. I looked at mum. She read my mind and abandoned her domestic duty, leaving the bin in the middle of the garden before shuffling back indoors.

It feels shit now to think that my own mum knew she embarrassed me. Not in the usual way teenagers are embarrassed by their parents. I was embarrassed by what she represented – a world that I'd tried to deny.

To make it easier for me, mum stopped making shutki on weekdays. Then, as I got older, I started hanging out with my friends on the weekend. Sometimes they would come and call for me. Mum avoided those weekends. Gradually, she made it less and less. I don't remember exactly when she stopped making shutki but I was glad. And now I feel bad. I probably should say sorry for being such a shit daughter but I don't.

FIRST THROUGH THE DOOR is Fedora hat-boy. Happily, he's not wearing his fedora hat. Though he could have made more effort. He arrives in a black leather bomber jacket. His jeans are ripped and his socks have pictures of Bart Simpson. Compared to Tall-boy, who was dressed to impress, Fedora hat-boy looks like he's popping to the shops for some biscuits. He's either super-casual, or he just doesn't care to be here. This is something of an insult as I've made an effort, wearing my pink embellished salwar kameez and matching bangles. I even applied my new Maybelline foundation especially for the occasion. I'm already unimpressed.

I now understand why his family sent a photo of Fedora hat-boy wearing a hat. He's got a clean-shaved head. This is unlikely to be a fashion statement and is probably a way of hiding his impending baldness. As a lack of hair is a deal breaker for many girls, Fedora hat-boy's family were playing it safe with a cunning disguise. He also seems to be a lot stouter than his photo suggested. And the muscular frame looks more like fat in person. Either his shirt was very well tailored in the photo or it's an old snap and he's since piled on the timber.

Interestingly, Fedora hat-boy arrives with just his mum. This is a much smaller party than Tall-boy's. My mum's annoyed as she's fried enough snacks to feed a family of six. It's also telling. His dad and older siblings stayed at home. The pessimist in me suggests that they couldn't be bothered either.

If I needed any more evidence that this wasn't a rishtaa for me, here it is – Fedora hat-boy is a pompous prick. When we're left alone for our obligatory chat, he initiates by asking me about my five-year plan. This sounds more like a job inter-view than any real job interview I've ever had. It also totally puts me on the spot.

I reply: "I haven't really thought about it."

Fedora hat-boy tuts and looks me square in the face, with an expression of disappointment. "You've not thought about it? So you don't know what you want to do with your life?"

He clearly hasn't met many Bengali girls. If he did, he'd understand that our main aim in life is to marry the man of our dreams. Yes, I love my PR job and I am perhaps more of a career girl than most but the only thing I'm certain of in five years is that I'll be hitched. At least I'm hoping so. And my work will fit around that. Not the other way round.

"What about *your* five-year plan?" I ask.

He then proceeds to bore me about how he wants to travel the world, listing the countries he hasn't seen and buy a house. Yep, he might think of himself as progressive but like any good Bengali boy, he still lives at home with mummy and daddy. At no point in his five-year plan does he mention getting married. Again, I'm wondering why he's even here.

The conversation continues in this vein. He talks about how he doesn't like to laze about on holiday and that he'd rather soak up some culture and do some sightseeing. I agree, saying there's more to holidays than sitting on the beach.

He responds with: "Oh I like sitting on the beach too. After all, the whole point of going on holiday is to relax."

It seems like whatever I say, this guy is determined to put forward a counter-argument. I don't even want to make eye contact with this knobhead. I lower my gaze, only to notice that he has a small hole in his sock at the big toe. Clearly he's spent so much money travelling that he's neglected his wardrobe.

Mum walks in with some vermicelli dessert, interrupting the awkward conversation. I'm relieved. I just want this visit to be over. Thankfully, like my first rishtaa meeting, the boy-girl chat is the last item on the agenda. In this case, it was a very short agenda as my family only had to entertain one other relative.

Before Fedora hat-boy is about to leave, his mum, a tiny-looking grey haired woman wearing a washed out beige saree, shuffles towards me and gives me a tight hug. I see her face close up. She's really old. Weathered by time. She looks at me for a long second. In her eyes there seems a sadness, almost a last-chance saloon sense of despair. Fedora hat-boy is the second youngest in his family and he's one of six. He's nearly 31 and something tells me that he isn't as keen to get married as his parents would like. This would explain the lack of sartorial effort and shitty attitude. The investigative journalist in me reckons that he's either got a white girlfriend, is gay, or a self-hating Asian. I bet he doesn't want an arranged marriage and is going along with things at his parents' wishes. However, by doing this, he's wasting other people's time, including mine.

It looks like I'm not the only one who sensed a bad attitude. Middle sis comes over to me after they've left. "He seemed like a bit of a knob, didn't he?"

I nod and agree.

Though mum doesn't fluently understand English, she can read body language like an expert. She sensed his arrogance too. After asking me what I think, she says: "Never mind, boy like that is waste of time. And he got no hair. I call Mr Choudhury first, before boy family have chance to say no. You no worry, you just eat these shomsha. We've got lots left."

The following weekend's rishtaa wasn't much more successful. But this was down to a much more shallow reason on my part. I could talk at length about the potential mother-in-law and how she was the polar opposite of Fedora hat-boy's mum. This mum was younger, probably in her late 40s / early 50s and looked much feistier. She eschewed the traditional hijab in favour of a stylish coiffed updo. Her eyebrows were plucked to oblivion and redrawn with a pencil.

As my mum would say, she looked like a modern cow. And what is the significance of this? Well, Bengali mums matter. Despite there being a widely held belief that ours is a patriarchal society, more often than not women rule the roost. They make the key decisions behind closed doors. So if the mum's a bitch, you're up shit creek. I know every country has the monster-in-law stories, but in our culture, the situation is worsened by the fact that you might have to live with your in-laws, at least in the early years of your marriage.

Every boy I've seen so far, including this one, lives with his mum and dad. That's quite the norm for unmarried Bengali boys, unless they live in a different city for work. The general unwritten rule seems to be that boys live at home initially, before moving into their own place within a year or two. As middle sis lived with the in-laws initially, I've come to accept that as the normal way of doing things.

Even if you end up in a place of your own, chances are that mummy-in-law will still be a looming presence. After all, it's well known that in Asian culture you don't just marry the boy, you marry the whole family too. And front and centre of that family is mummy dearest.

Bengali mums tend to fall into two distinct categories, each with their own specific challenges. If they're old, like Fedora hat-boy's mum, chances are they'll be less feisty and bothersome as they often have their own ailments to deal with. However, there may be a greater expectation for you to pick up the baton domestically.

If they're young, like this rishtaa's mum, it could go one of two ways. They'll either be a really cool, modern mum who understands that you need your marital space and leaves you and their son to get on with your lives. They might even become more like a friend than a mother-in-law. However, there is also a very real chance that they'll be strong-willed and overbearing. It's likely that they'll have an opinion on everything, from your choice of career to your way of cooking and how you raise your children.

Judging by the looks of this mum, with her 'don't mess with me' face and harsh eyebrows, I would bet she fell into the latter category. That may sound judgmental but without the luxury of getting to know someone and their family over a period of years, the cover of the book is all you can go by. And quite often, the cover is an accurate depiction of the story inside.

There was also the small issue about his 'management' role. He was a store manager in a clothes shop. So yes, he's technically in management, just not the type that I thought. As an academic and occupational snob, this doesn't sit very well with me.

If this all sounds terribly shallow, brace yourself for the next bit. His mum, his job and everything else pales in comparison to one thing I can't get past... he is tiny. Like, really tiny. His biodata says 5ft 6in but I'm calling bullshit.

There's no denying that he's shorter than me. But more to the point, he's more petite than I am. His small frame makes him look like a little boy. He's wearing a charcoal-coloured pin-stripe suit, the jacket looks far too big with its 80s shoulder pads and the skinny pink tie fails to add maturity. He looks like a schoolboy. Despite him being four years older than me, I could pass for his big sister. And I'm only a size eight and look very young myself. With age and childbirth I'll likely only get bigger, whereas I suspect he'll always be petite. Many girls don't mind being larger than their man but I couldn't settle for a life-time of looking like a big old bird next to a teenager.

The worst part is that this boy actually sounded normal. He's not travelled yet – perhaps airport security don't think he's old enough to fly without a parent – but he'd like to "with the right person," he tells me with a shy smile. It turns out he'd like that person to be me.

To my mortification, he asked if he could take my number while we were having our one-to-one chat. "It might be easier to talk that way," he reasoned.

I nearly fell off my chair. Surely that's against the rules at stage one? I'm not sure whether to be offended or impressed with his request.

Unsure of what to say, I pull out the prudish Bengali-girl card, muttering: "Oh, I wouldn't mind but shouldn't we con-sult our parents first? It's probably the right thing to do."

Like parental permission has ever stopped me before. And *I wouldn't mind*??? What a cop out.

After Small-boy had left, mum, big sis and I convene around the table with the leftover samosas for a debrief. Unanimously, we agreed that Small-boy was too small.

Mum, politically incorrect as ever, says: "He wasn't even full-sized man. You'll get small kids."

There are so many things that are offensive about her statement but I'm too tired to correct her.

Big sis chimes in with: "And did you see the mum in her low-cut saree blouse? Her boobs were practically out on the dining table."

"Dooro!" mum hisses, stifling a laugh at the same time. "Your dad will hear you!"

"Oh relax, he's got the Bangla news blasting in the front room, he won't hear a thing. And there was a lot of boob. I wasn't sure where to look," big sis argues.

My sister is clearly exaggerating. Though there was more dimply cleavage than I would have liked to see on a Sunday afternoon. And yes, big sis is just as unfiltered as mum. It must be a Bengali immigrant thing.

Then we hear an annoying teenage voice: "He was smaller than me!" Little sis sniggers.

I didn't realise she was in the room. She must have been playing on her phone in the corner. Bless her, she's trying to get involved in the girl talk. She pulls up a chair, and we all spend the evening talking and laughing about the last two rishtaas. Big sis reminds us of her rishtaas in Bangladesh, which I'd long forgotten about.

"Now let's see. There was lanky Larry, baby face and heffalump," she recalls.

"Which one was heffalump?" I ask.

"You know... the hefty one. Not that I can talk now," she sighs, looking down at her not-so-skinny frame.

Mum seizes the opportunity for a life lesson: "See, never make fun anyone. No-one can say how you end up, or with who you end up."

"Oh, sorry. What was it you said about today's rishtaa? He's not a full-sized man?" Big sis teases.

Mum has the perfect answer: "I wasn't making funny, I was speaking truth."

"Well anyway," big sis continues, "this little fella is quite the catch compared to some of the bobby dazzlers that came my way."

"They not all been bad," mum argues. "You just too fussy."

"I don't think turning down heffalump was fussy, mum," says big sis. "I hardly had Bollywood heroes knocking on my door. In fact, all the women in our family are great at the art of compromise, apart from Rashda. Some of the boys she turned down... I wouldn't have said no."

"Dooro!" says mum. "Have shame."

"I'm only being honest. That girl's still got eyes on her and she knows it. I bet she'll be all dolled up like a queen at her brother's wedding. I'm glad I won't be there to sit near her."

"Oh stop! If you jealous, then lose weight!" Mum is supportive as always.

"I will. Diet starts in January," she says, dipping her third samosa into a pool of ketchup.

Big sis has never been so funny. She's usually got a stiff upper lip, playing up to her first-born role. I forgot that she's actually quite witty. Through her banter, she's reminding me that she's been through it and that there *is* a happy ending. It's a welcome gesture, as it's easy to think that everyone else had it good. Big sis, with her big house, kind husband and cute kids, seems to have it all. Yet she had to go through her fair share of uncomfortable rishtaa meetings before she met my brother-in-law. Despite them having fewer opportunities to meet pre-marriage due to more strict formalities back home, it's plain to see that they are made for each other. If ever there was a poster couple for arranged marriages, surely they were it.

I'm glad to have a talking point with big sis. I'm glad we're all on the same page. We don't say it out aloud but we all know that this arranged marriage business is one big hilarious headfuck. If it wasn't so funny, I'd be quite sad.

However, despite the giggles, I'm becoming all too aware that time is marching on and I'm no closer to finding the one. With each failed rishtaa meeting, each date, each disappointment, I'm beginning to wonder if the one actually exists.

# 6th December, I hate weddings

I hate weddings. I HATE weddings. I bloody hate them.

OK, SO HATE'S A BIT of a strong word. I don't *hate* weddings. There are many great aspects to them. I love the food (though I'm still mourning the departure of the tandoori leg of chicken that was once the standard starter. No amount of samosas, seekh kebabs and masala fish will ever replace that red-dyed, charred chicken). The dressing up part is fun too, even if my execution isn't always pretty. I'm also acutely aware that weddings are a necessary weapon in the single lady's arsenal. You simply have to attend them, to see and to be seen.

But they're also a painful reminder of my unmarried status. When you're invited to the nuptials of a boy that's three years younger than you... well, that's just rubbing it in.

The boy in question is my cousin Iqbal, Rashda's younger brother. So I guess that's what auntie was stressed about when she came over. She perhaps hoped that her 23-year-old newly graduated son wouldn't rush into marriage.

"It's a love marriage," mum informed me when we received the wedding invite. "I shouldn't talk this with you... but... he met girl at uni-barsity. So Rashda ma not happy. She want him be doctor and focus on studies, not girl. Plus his older sister not yet married. Why he jump queue?"

Obviously Iqbal had other ideas beyond medicine. As the family wanted to avoid any conflict with their youngest and only son, he got his way.

Initially, I didn't want to attend. The wedding is in Wolverhampton, so it'll be a mission and I'll no doubt have a makeup meltdown en route. I'm also the designated driver (read: only driver in my family), so I have the tricky task of driving in heels and a saree and negotiating black ice, three things rarely conducive to operating a vehicle. At least middle sis and her lot will be there, so there'll be some company. I reckon mum will ditch me for Auntie Jusna and her lady gang.

The day before the wedding I head to Selfridges for a beauty tutorial. I will not be beaten by a bad makeup job this time. My appointment is with Daniel, a very pretty makeup artist with glowing skin and a flawless highlight. Straight away I feel like I'm in good hands.

"What look d'ya wanna go for, love?" He asks while priming my face.

I don't dare say lighter than my natural skin tone for fear of opening a racial can of worms.

"Oh, just a little glowy. Nothing too drastic."

"What's the occasion, love?"

"It's for a wedding."

"An Indian wedding?"

"Well, Bengali but yes."

"Oh, I'd die to go to one of them. It's the outfits. They're *sooooo* glamorous. But if you're going to a wedding, we might have to up the ante on the makeup."

"Erm, right ok. But I don't want to go overboard..."

"Don't you worry love, yer in safe hands with me. I'll do a little smokey eye."

"Oh I'm not sure if that suits –,"

"Right, you're all primed," Daniel interjects. "Now let's get colour-matching."

This is my least favourite bit of any makeup tutorial. Daniel reaches for three different foundation shades, swatching each on my jawline.

"Right, well this one is right for your skin tone," Daniel declares, pointing at a deep brown shade which is clearly too dark.

"Are you sure? I was thinking the one a shade lighter."

"Oh no love, that's the same shade I use. You'd look silly."

I look up from my makeup chair for a closer look. Daniel's makeup may look great but I notice a telltale sign – there's a distinct line around his jaw where the makeup ends and his real skin is exposed. Needless to say, the two don't match. He's doing the opposite of what most Asian girls do.

Daniel gets to work on my foundation, using the darker shade he's chosen. But he gets a bit trigger-happy and goes ahead with a smokey eye. He hands me the mirror.

"Oh my... I look... umm," I don't have the words. It looks like I've applied mud to my face. The heavy grey eye makeup isn't helping either. It's all wrong.

"Love, you're *glow-ing*. That's what you wanted, wasn't it?" Daniel looks pissed off. You should never challenge an artiste's work.

"Yeah... I think I just need to get used to it. What was that shade of foundation again?"

"Chocolate."

I buy a foundation brush from Daniel, just to get out of paying the £20 tutorial fee. I then head to a rival department store to buy the same brand of foundation, only two shades lighter.

THE DRIVE DOWN TO WOLVERHAMPTON is traumatic. Google Maps screws me over and we end up going up a tram lane in the city. I'm not even sure if cars are allowed to be there. I skid on the ice. Plus my parents are the worst people to be in a car with when you don't know where you're going.

Dad's concerned. "*Lost nee?*"

"No, I'm not lost, dad. We're ok."

"Sure? Stop and ask someone?" mum unhelpfully suggests.

"I can't just stop in the middle of a busy road!"

"It's ok, just pull here."

"Mum, that's a bus stop. I'll get a fine."

"How bout here?" Mum points towards a road clearly marked with a 'no entry' sign.

I ignore her.

"I don-no if I should have worn this fanjabi. Is peach a lady colour?" Dad clearly has bigger issues at large.

"No it's fine. I told you, this is dress code. I wear peach too. Only your daughter no wear it," says mum in disappointment. "I still doh-no why you has to wear blue. Always be different.

"Mum, I don't own peach anything. And I'm not going to spend hundreds on a saree I'll only wear once."

"You too stingy! Never make effort," mum moans.

"I don't want to look silly. Like I wearing lady clothes," says dad.

"Acha! So we go back home now, just to change to man clothes? Silly... Your fanjabi more orange than peach anyhow. Don't you want to match with your sister and her perfect family?"

Dad bows his head like a scolded schoolboy. I can see him in the passenger seat adjusting his brown waistcoat as if to hide his peachy-orange kurta.

"Eh-heh. We getting late. Still lost?"

"No dad, it's fine."

"I tell you, just ask someone. And no drive so fast, you cause accident. So much ice on road."

"Mum you're making things worse! Just let me drive. Who's idea was it for a winter wedding, anyway?"

"Iqbal of course. If your Auntie Jusna had choice, there be no wedding at all."

There's a precious moment of silence.

Dad sighs. "Eh-heh. Probably lost but this girl too stubborn."

How I wish bratty sis were with us. At least she could take charge of directions.

AS I TAKE MY SEAT AT the wedding, I'm pretty pleased with how I look. Daniel may have coloured me not-beautiful but I did learn a thing or two about highlighting and contouring. I skipped the smokey eye, instead opted for a muted gold-beige look finished with a slick of liquid eyeliner. It complements my blue saree with gold thread work. Ordinarily blue is a colour I would avoid like the plague, as I've always thought it was darkening. But this unusual shade of royal blue seems to work. And my biggest secret? False lashes. Not the exaggerated bridal lashes which could take someone else's eye out. The understated kind that leaves people guessing if you're even wearing falsies or you're just born with it.

Hair is simple and straight, no faffing around with back-combing or curls that give up after an hour. I'm not sure why it took me this long to discover that less really is more.

Even middle sis is impressed. "You look good. Blue is your colour. I think you'll get noticed today," she winks.

She's clad in a pale peach gown with delicate beading. She looks like a fairy princess, so if anyone's going to get noticed...

I look around. The massive banqueting suite, which used to be a mill, is already teeming with guests and we've arrived early. The venue staff are hurriedly unfolding more tables and adding green satin ribbons to the backs of chairs they weren't expecting to use. The venue has capacity for hundreds and they still need to lay more tables. I don't see how I'll get spotted in this crowd. I also think there might be a fistfight over the food.

My beady eye makes a discovery – elusive Auntie Fatima. I didn't expect her to be here but then I forgot that she bloody knows EVERYONE. I bet her and my real Auntie Jusna have had a good old gossip about me. I reckon Auntie knows more about the Tall-boy situation than I do.

Auntie Fatima enters through the gold-pillared altar-style entrance and begins looking around for a table. She has someone with her – a girl about my age, clad in a burgundy brocade saree with matching hijab. Auntie Fatima spots me and there's an awkward moment when we both lock eyes. Her expression is notable – if her hazel eyes could talk, they'd be saying *oh shit*.

I'm not the only one who's spotted her, as mum, nestled between middle sis and my niece, almost flings herself over our table to make a beeline for my pretend auntie. Clearly mum still wants closure on the whole Tall-boy saga.

Middle sis whispers to me: "That looks awkward. What do you think they're talking about?"

"Well, I'm guessing mum's skirting around the subject of my single status."

"Why does she bother? Clearly auntie Fatima is crap at matchmaking, anyway. Didn't she go quiet about that last guy, the tall one?"

"Well she only ever introduced one guy and, yeah, we never heard back."

"Mum needs to get over it though and stop acting like that lad was your only option. I mean, if you weren't bothered, why is mum so obsessed?"

I'm glad middle sis is oblivious to the extent of my initial disappointment. But it's also a bit sad how I can't share my true feelings with my own sister.

Auntie Fatima, her mystery companion and mum come over to our table. I'm overlooked in favour of middle sis, who's greeted with a big hug.

"Oh! It's been so long since I last saw you," auntie Fatima says to my sis in her broad Lancashire accent. "Each year you get prettier."

She gestures towards her guest, this time speaking in Bengali: "This here is my niece. She's come from 'desh and is staying with me."

There's a bit of an awkward silence, before desperately mundane niceties fill the void.

"So, how's your father?"

"He's good. He's sat with the other mesaabs," middle sis gestures with her head to the other side of the makeshift wall where the men are sat.

Such flimsy partitions, precariously held together with office dividers, make no sense to me. Everyone – man, woman and child – congregates together in the end, anyway.

Auntie Fatima's niece is incredibly slim, thinner than me and has big almond eyes. She smiles a dimple-y smile and says: "Assalamu alaikum."

Finally, I'm noticed. "Are you areet love? I haven't seen you in ages."

It seems like everyone that flakes on me turns it around like *I'm* the one hiding.

"Have you lost weight?" Auntie Fatima asks me.

"Not that I'm aware."

"Don't lose anymore weight. You're skinny enough already love. It doesn't suit you," auntie Shit-ima helpfully adds. "Where's the little lady?"

"She's at home revising," I reply, stretching out the crisp white napkin which was carefully folded into a fan. I wish it were a real fan right now.

"Oh, you got to keep up with the studies. Nowadays you need to be well qualified. For work and marriage."

Is she taunting me?

I feel my cheeks flushing and head get hot, like I'm going to combust. I've tried so hard to forget Tall-boy and let sleeping dogs lie. I thought I'd gotten over it. I thought I was past car-ing. But seeing Auntie Fatima in person and *still* not being able to ask her outright what's happened is unexpectedly paralysing. This fake politeness that we have to put on is pissing me off.

"Assalamu Alaikum everyone. Can you please be seated? Food will be served shortly," a voice mumbles on the PA.

Saved by the starters.

Auntie Fatima and her niece say their goodbyes and go and find a couple of seats. They'll be bloody lucky. There's no seating plan and the venue is now groaning with hungry guests who probably don't even know the couple in question.

"What was that about?" Middle sis asks, once the coast is clear. "You look so miffed."

"That's coz I am. I hate the way we always have to pussyfoot around things. Aunty Fatima never told us what happened with that rishtaa. She just buggered off. She got our hopes up. She got *my* hopes up and then said bugger all. And now she's acting like it doesn't matter. Like it never happened. Like she didn't ever introduce a boy to me that I may have, just maybe, have considered marrying."

Middle sis tries to conceal a smirk: "Oh, come on, you're not that bothered are you? I mean, you only met him once."

"That's fucking irrelevant! In Bengali terms that's like... like the equivalent of six dates. And yes, I am bothered. Or at least I was bothered. I'm not supposed to say these things but I didn't have loads of options like you. I *still* don't have loads of options like you."

Thank goodness Bengali weddings are overcrowded affairs. It means that this conversation, which really should have been saved for a more private setting, could be had so publicly.

My sister's face turns solemn. "Awww babe. I didn't realise you felt like that. And you have got options. For what it's worth, I don't think he was all that. And his mum seemed like a right miserable old hag. I bet she'd give you grief."

Mum interjects: "Dooro! What you talking about? People hear you."

"Just Auntie Fatima the flake," says middle sis.

"Snake more like," mum hisses, surprising us both.

Middle sis leans into mum. "What do you mean?"

"Well, she's brought her niece over from 'desh. I bet it's her job to get her married to Beet-ish boy. So she's putting all opportunities that way. Including our opportunity."

Middle sis sees the shock on my face. "Mum, you don't know that."

"I'm ma, I know these things."

I don't say anything. Mum could be right, though it's hard to believe. Would Auntie Fatima really scupper things to get her niece married? Surely, if she told both parties that the other side isn't interested, she'd be scared of getting caught? Then again, she knows how polite we are about these things, tiptoeing around the issue, she probably knows she'll never get rumbled. Society dictates that even if there was foul play, we wouldn't be able to say anything. It's just not how it works. But even if she did tell Tall-boy's family that we weren't interested and did the same to us, it doesn't mean that they'd necessarily opt for Auntie Fatima's niece from Bangladesh as a backup option. Then again, his sister-in-law is from Bangladesh. Maybe his mum wanted the same for him. Perhaps *he* wanted that for himself. Too many questions, not enough answers.

An old lady shuffles over to mum, interrupting my confusing internalised investigation. I've never met her before. After a few pleasantries, she gets down to the hot topic – me.

"So you gon get her married? Time's passing, no?"

I'm sitting right here. She doesn't care. I pretend not to listen and turn my attention to the wedding favour – a tiny, drawstring bag made of bridal red mesh. It contains two Quality Street chocolates and a date fruit. Nice touch. I see drawstring party favours are all the rage at weddings these days. Must make a note of that, if I ever manage to get married.

Mum responds to the nosey lady in her usual way: "Inshallah, we're looking. Tell us if hear of any nice groom, yes?"

Mum knows that most of these women won't ever come good. Everyone wants to pry but nobody wants to help. Perhaps it's force of habit or false hope that makes her ask, anyway.

I am more than ready to go home. Despite the compere's insistence on getting everyone seated, the starters haven't even arrived.

Finally, after 45 minutes, a stream of waiting staff clad in head-to-toe black uniform, emerge with silver trays in each hand. Perhaps hearing our groaning stomachs, they pick up the pace, tossing the trays onto our table like they're silver Frisbees. There's seekh kebab, samosas and lamb chops.

This is where the Bangladeshi politeness ends. It's a free-for-all. We're seated on a table of eight and two ladies have joined our table, just in time for the food. They don't speak to us but dive into the starters, piling two of each item onto their plates. It's only when they spot my nephew and niece, hungry and eager, that they pass the tray round to the small children.

My nephew loads up three samosas into his tray and proceeds to only bite a corner of each. There are only two samosas left.

"You and mum have them. I'll eat his leftovers," says middle sis.

Just then, the groom makes his way through the gold altar thingy, followed by his entourage (family) and takes his seat at a long table at the front of the hall. He's dressed rather regally, in a black velvet sherwani embellished with diamante stonework, which adds volume to his slim boyish frame. The bling theme follows right through to his turban, which is of the same velvet variety and decorated with a sparking brooch, which sprouts a peacock feather. It's a bit much for my liking. If this is what *he's* dressed like, I can't wait to see the bride.

Though his look is very over the top, Iqbal *kind of* pulls it off. He's been genetically blessed with the same fair skin, dimples and dazzling smile of his eldest sister, Rashda. It's funny as I've always seen him as a kid. It's weird how he's morphed into a handsome, if not overdressed, groom.

I spot people busting through the makeshift walls, as the men and boys start milling around in what was the ladies only area. I guessed the partition wouldn't last long but ordinarily we at least stay segregated until the desserts are served.

"I wonder where Rashda is? She's probably hoping to make a grand entrance. Even at her own brother's wedding, I'm sure she's not above a spot of upstaging," huffs Middle sis. As the two standout beauties in our family, they've always been competitive. I guess the decades of comparison didn't help.

Iqbal's mum and other sister are sat next to him. Maybe Rashda *is* going to make it about her, by entering with her husband and kids. The colour scheme – which I flouted and middle sis adhered to – is peach. She'll wear it well.

Finally, Rashda arrives but without the ceremony we expected. Instead, she shuffles in, being pulled along by her daughter, while her five-year-old son is tugging at her arm to leave. She's wearing a rather drab olive green saree, void of much decoration. While I can get away with shunning the peach dress code, I figured that the sister of the groom would have to conform.

No sooner have we eaten our starters, that the mains start arriving with the same sense of urgency. My niece hasn't even finished her seekh kebab, before the silver trays of starters disappear and are quickly replaced by steaming bowls of rice. Three curries are thrown down in quick succession – the standard staples of meat, chicken and veg.

The ladies sat at our table are grumbling about the service and how rushed everything is. But I'm glad. I just want to eat and go.

As we're chowing down our mains and giving ourselves indigestion, the groom takes to the stage. It's time for photos. He sits on his makeshift gold and red velvet throne, like some Saudi Prince surveying his subjects.

Family after family join the queue to have their pictures taken on the throne. I can't be arsed. I'd rather wait until the bride joins him, then I'll take a pic with the happy couple. However, mum loves a photo shoot and strong arms my sis into joining her for a photo call with the dashing boy-groom and his smug mum. They've got a long wait though, as many girls around my own age are taking their sweet time, posing for rishtaa-ready photos. Some aren't even sitting near the groom and instead are standing alone near the golden floor vases, looking picture perfect. This is clearly where I've been going wrong. All these years I should have been using other people's wedding stage's as my own personal photo studio.

I'm left with the kids for company.

"You not taking a picture?" I hear a voice from behind me.

It's Rashda. Close up, I can see she's lost weight. Her face looks gaunt.

"Nah, I'll just wait for the bride to arrive."

"Well it might be awhile, this wedding is nothing if not *looong*," she does a fake yawn.

"Oh, I can tell from all the details. I'm particularly impressed with the chocolate fountain. It must have been an organisational nightmare for you though, being in the thick of it."

Rashda smiles but the glee fails to reach her eyes. "I wasn't too involved."

I'm surprised she got out of it. Usually the siblings bear the brunt of the wedding planning. I remember when middle sis was getting married, big sis had to take care of all the details like booking the wedding hall, choosing the menu and even arranging the bridal limo. Basically, she was lumbered with what would usually be the son's job. Dad just arranged for the Imam from the local mosque to officiate. With Iqbal being the only son, I assumed such duties would fall upon Rashda's dainty shoulders.

"I guess having kids was your get out of jail card," I joke.

"Something like that."

"Well, it all looks fab, anyway. Does it take you back to your wedding day?"

"Not so much. Mine feels like so long ago. A lot has changed in the ten years since. My wedding was grand for its time but this is on another level. I mean, look at all these extra things!"

Rashda grabs a handful of fresh rose petals off the table, before letting them slip through her fingers and float back down, like a floral waterfall. "My brother arrived in a Ferrari. His chavvy mates hired souped-up cars too. And wait till you see the bride. You'd think she's robbed a jewellery shop!"

I've never really seen this catty side of Rashda. She's normally so... prim. I rather like this bitchiness.

She leans closer to me, as if to impart some age-old wisdom: "When it's your turn to get married, don't do any of this crap. Keep it simple and save your money. Focus on the rest of your life, not just one day which is basically about impressing everyone else."

"That's if I get married. At this rate, I'm not so sure. I'm sure Auntie's told you about my failed rishtaas."

"Mum doesn't tell me much these days, so I'm not in the loop of anyone's rishtaas," she says.

I look at her, surprised. I always thought she was her mum's biggest confidante.

Rashda quickly adds: "And I like it that way. My life is busy enough without sticking my beak in other people's business. But honestly, as someone who's had the big fat Bengali wedding, I can speak with experience. Don't get wrapped up in one day. Focus on the guy. That's the most important thing. And as for failed rishtaas, well that's their loss. You'll get snapped up in no time. Just make sure the right one snaps you up."

Auntie Jusna comes over, ignores me and says: "Why are you sat here when there's photos to be taken? The bride's about to enter the stage."

"Ok I'm coming," Rashda replies before turning to me. "Right, you heard mum, so come with me. The bride's here, so no excuses. We can't have you looking like that and not taking your pic."

Luckily the queue for photos has shortened, as most people have turned their attention to the desserts, which are just being served. It's gulab jamun and ice cream, the best blend of east and west.

I'm tempted to abandon my place in the queue but mum's read my mind: "You can eat later. Let get nice family shot with bride-groom."

I approach the stage for the obligatory family pic. Rashda wasn't lying. The bride is weighed down by jewels. She has a diamante head piece, a three-tiered gold necklace (no doubt gifted by the groom's side) and armfuls of glittering bangles. The intricate henna-art on her hands is hidden underneath the heavy diamante hand-pieces she is wearing.

Beneath the bling and heavy makeup, I can barely see her face. She's probably about the same age as Iqbal as they met at university but she looks older, with a curvy, womanly figure. I sit next to her for the photos, middle sis takes a seat next to the groom, while mum sits on the adjacent golden chaise lounge with two the little ones.

"You look gorgeous," I tell the bride, as it seems like the right thing to say.

"Awww thank yaaaoow," she says in a strong Midlands accent.

"So how you feeling?"

"I'm or-roit," she says. "A bit nervous but okay."

"Bet you can't wait to take all this bling off," I say.

"Oh I don't mind. I only get dolled up like this once in me life, so might as well milk it."

And that is how I'm different to most girls. While she's loving getting dolled up for the biggest day of her life, I opt for comfort over aesthetics, always.

Once middle sis' kids start running feral and getting chocolate marshmallows all over their cute little outfits, we know it's time to leave. We locate dad, who looks terribly self-conscious in his peach number (all the other men his age were wearing muted tones), and say our long goodbyes.

While mum tries to get middle sis to stop by our house en route to Bradford, I spot Auntie Fatima parading her niece around like some human show-and-tell. Then mum, having failed to persuade middle sis to take a cup of tea detour, turns and gives Auntie Fatima a big enthusiastic wave.

That's the most annoying thing of all. Mum's seething at Auntie Fatima now. Give it a few months and they'll be friends again.

# 25<sup>th</sup> December, Familiar faces and new ones too

It's times like this I'm glad we don't celebrate Christmas. I'm sorry to sound blasphemous but if we did, all the boys on my online dating site would bugger off for two weeks to spend time with their families, seriously delaying my efforts to find a husband. Instead, digital activity in the Muslim matrimonial world is just as fervent as ever. In fact, I've discovered that these websites are a guilty pleasure – nobody talks about them but everybody uses them.

I'm fairly cloak and dagger, with my unassuming username and hidden photo but others are more open. I stumbled upon Small-boy's profile picture. He's still claiming to be 5ft 6in. But I wish him well and hope he finds the tiny princess of his dreams. He was a nice boy but I just didn't fancy spending my life wearing a waist-shrinking corset and flat shoes to avoid looking huge in his presence. In true irony, he was the guy that was most interested in me. His family called Mr Choudhury straight after they visited us, wanting to know if I want to take things further. Mum had to say a polite no. Isn't that always the way? The one you don't fancy is an eager beaver but the one you do isn't so forthcoming.

Speaking of which...

Tall-boy is also on this site. This means that even if Auntie Fatima had pushed her niece in his direction, he's not marrying her. By the looks of things, he's still very much single. Rather brazenly, he uses his full name and his picture is available for all to see. There's no denying it's him. It's the same familiar smile, and the dark, shiny skin. I think he might even be wearing the suit that he wore to meet me. I don't blame him, it's a good look.

Now, if this was a Bollywood movie, or a romantic novel, this is where the love story would reach its pivotal point. I'd message him, or he would contact me and our stars would align. It was meant to be, like his father said. And as we didn't quite match through the formal rishtaa setting, this is where we'd find each other.

I would have finally understood why I never heard from him or his family. And there would be a dramatic reason. Either:

a) He was involved in a car accident and has been co-matose all this time. When he woke, the first word he said was my name.

Or

b) His resting bitch face mum didn't like me. She'd rather he married a girl from Bangladesh, like Auntie Fatima's niece. But he liked me, so he was disowned and carted out of the family home. He'd been spending all this time making his way back to me, by foot. Oh, and he was hoping to increase his chances of finding me by setting up an online profile at the same time.

Alas, this isn't a love story. This is real life. In fact, it's my life. And that shit doesn't happen to me.

I contemplated sending Tall-boy a message. The temptation to reach out was huge. Because, if nothing else, I wanted proper closure. I wanted to know the reason behind the silence. Did Auntie Fatima put a spanner in the works? Was it his mum? Or was he simply not interested? My pride was hurt after that first rishtaa and the ensuing ghosting. I was disappointed in myself for misreading the signals and daring to get excited. And deep down, a part of me *still* would like things to work out with Tall-boy, as he's the best I've seen so far.

However, the bottom line is, whatever the reason for not hearing from Tall-boy's family, the fact remains that *he* never got back in touch. If he wanted to see me again, he should have been man enough to make it happen. After all, isn't *he* the one looking to get married? This leads me to conclude that he's clearly not for me. That's the best closure I'll ever have. I didn't message Tall-boy. Instead I closed that chapter for good and I won't mention him again.

As the world of online dating moves at a breakneck speed, I've moved on (again) and am messaging a new boy. Now that might make me look like a total flooze but given that none of these meetings were actual relationships, I'm entitled to get a wriggle on. Also, I'm a 26-year-old Bengali girl who is heading into the New Year as a single woman. So I damn well will continue hunting.

Anyway, like all my online dalliances, this boy reached out to me, as I'm too old-school to make the first move. He's done all the pursuing and by this I mean he's been contacting me regularly. We've even unlocked pictures at mutual request and he was chivalrous enough to share his first.

I opened his picture with mixed feelings. I was doing my best to manage my own expectations but was getting overpowered by pangs of hope. As the photo finally loads, I'm glad I kept my glass a little empty. He stands tall in the pic, with his hands behind his back and his legs further apart than necessary, kind of like a bodyguard manning an exclusive venue. Underneath his black suit is a red paisley print waistcoat, which complements the rug on which he's standing. He obviously likes the outfit, as he's enhanced its prominence by puffing his chest out with pride. The photo looks like it was meant for such hunting purposes, and I bet his mum orchestrated the shoot.

He's not unattractive but my younger self may have turned him down. His hair looks quite thinned out and spiky and he has fairer skin than me. I know this goes against my rule but I think I'm prettier so it evens things out. His eyebrows are fine and wispy, almost non-existent. This makes his brow-bone look even more prominent. On the plus side, he's a good age (28) and for Bengali standards, he's pretty tall, standing at 5ft 9in. His build is regular – not particularly slim, but not fat either.

This guy also lives the optimum distance from me. By that I mean it's a half-hour drive from his parents house to mine. That makes it an easy commute but not close enough to bump into each other frequently if things don't work out.

From conversations, I've learnt that his older brother has flown the nest and he's got a younger brother still living at home, along with two sisters. Outside of the family home, he seems to have friends and a social life of sorts. This is a big plus and something that Shy-boy lacked. He even plays squash once a week.

That's the good stuff. Here's what's not so good...

He's been to university and studied law but he's not the barrister of my dreams. He works as a paralegal. As I've got a pretty lucrative PR job, I'm probably earning more than him. Call me old-fashioned but I don't think I'd be happy being the breadwinner, given that I'll be the one to have kids and take a step back in my career later on.

He also doesn't have a car. I remember Reena had a boyfriend who didn't drive when we were at university. She was forever complaining about having to be the chauffeur. And despite my forward thinking ways, I'm a simple girl who appreciates chivalry. That includes picking up the tab and picking me up. Or at least doing *some* driving. Given that I'm a bit nervous behind the wheel, I always assumed one perk of getting married would be that I'd do less driving, not more.

Finally and there's no nice way of putting this... he's got two photos on his profile. In the first he's standing tall, chest puffed and not smiling. The second is a close-up shot where he's grinning away. And I notice his teeth. They're so... small. I know that's a weird observation but I can't see past them. They're like the baby teeth Ben Affleck had before his *Armageddon* makeover (Google it). He's smiling widely in his picture (though said smile doesn't really go that wide) with his thin lips peeled back to reveal just visible gnashers.

I consult my unofficial dating guru Sophia about this Small tooth-boy. I share my concerns about his work and his lack of wheels but I leave out my more shallow quibbles. She's constantly banging on about personality over looks, so I don't want to get another lecture from her about beauty being more than skin deep. I have to call Sophia as she's been rubbish at meeting up lately. She always has stuff on with her husband, which serves as an unwelcome and unnecessary reminder that as a singleton, I have much more time on my hands.

Sophia, pragmatic as ever, tackles each of my concerns. "Hon, look at it this way – a paralegal role leaves room for professional development and he may well train to become a lawyer. He just might not have got round to it."

I note that I must ask him about this when we meet, without sounding too pushy, of course.

On the issue of driving, Sophia agrees that it's not ideal as it's nice for the guy to get behind the wheel (I think all us girls are old-fashioned like that). "But on balance, all these things are insignificant if he's a nice guy. And you'll only know that if you meet him. So go and bloody meet him!"

Sophia sounds exhausted. My endless manhunt and constant need for counsel must be wearing thin. I really should consult other friends about boys in the future – spread the load and all that. However, she makes a good point. I've hardly got a queue of men outside my door. The pretend marriage events died down over December and Small tooth-boy is keen. So we exchange numbers and start speaking on the phone.

He tends to call me after work, on his way home on the bus. Part of me wonders whether he's not that invested if he's calling me to pass the time en route home. The other side of me wonders whether his family is quite strict, so he can't be heard talking to a girl on his mobile. But my more pragmatic self decides to shut up and stop over-analysing.

Having spoken a few times, I'm glad to report that he has more conversation than Shy-boy. I've gauged that he's not completely stuck for words. We talk about work, though he refers to it as just a job that pays his way. He mentions his home life – he sits firmly in the middle of the sibling tree.

I purposely ask him about his plans for the evening, as I've got something to talk about beyond eating and bitching for a change. I'm attending boxercise classes, partly in a bid to keep fit and mainly to have a discussion point on dates.

Then, during one of our conversations, he comes out with it: "It's great talking to you, but it would be even better to meet now, if you're up for it. It doesn't have to be anything major, we could get coffee."

I wonder whether to say yes immediately. He's been elusive at times. Sometimes he won't reply to my message for a whole day. I don't know if he's playing hard to get or is just busy. In response, I find myself doing the same, and not replying straight away. I know it's petty but, if he's playing games, I have no choice but to partake. However, I decide that I should stop dithering and meet him, as time is of the essence.

Also, after my double-whammy rishtaa failing, I'm just glad to see someone outside of the formal family setting. Mum will also be relieved that she doesn't need to batch-fry any samosas. After Small-boy and his family left, mum realised that she's got about six samosas left in the freezer. She has to make more from scratch. If nothing else, mum can't wait for me to get married to put an end to perfect strangers eating her out of house and home.

Anyway, if it doesn't work out with Small tooth-boy, at least I'll get a free hot chocolate out of it.

# 29<sup>th</sup> December, Who said chivalry is dead?

S o I didn't get a free hot chocolate.

I find myself conflicted by chivalry. On one hand, I kind of feel sorry for the boys. They have to do ALL the legwork. They have to hold the door open, do the driving but, most importantly, they have to pay for everything.

OK, so they don't *have to* but society *expects* them to.

I'm constantly giving Julia unsolicited advice about *occasionally* picking up the tab with guys she's dating. She has this rule where she wants the boy to foot the bill, all the time. Even when she's been seeing someone for a few months, she sees it as his duty to pay for dinner on the 20<sup>th</sup> date.

Whereas I like to think I'm a bit more reasonable. As a 21<sup>st</sup> century British-Bengali girl, I think it's good to show a guy that you're not expecting to be a kept woman. There's nothing wrong with paying the bill on the third or fourth date, or surprising them with a gift, without hoping for something sparkly in return. In fact, I particularly feel sorry for the boys who are doing the online dating or arranged marriage thing, therefore going on lots of first dates. They must wonder, *how many bitches do I need to buy dinner for before I find a wife?*

It can indeed turn into a very expensive affair.

However, I like *some* chivalry.

I don't expect to pay the bill on the first date. But that's exactly what I've just done. As I wrap up my date with this guy, I find myself light of pocket and heavy of heart. My meeting with Shy-boy might have been awkward but this encounter really took the piss.

Firstly, I risk being spotted by a relative as Small tooth-boy requests that we meet in the city centre. As he doesn't drive, central Manchester is easier for him to get to than my usual obscure industrial estate Caffe Nero. This is not so great for me, as the many one-way streets in town get me all in a bother. I leave home early, mainly because mum and dad have gone out on the bus to the cash and carry to buy some chicken, so it's my chance to escape without mum's twenty questions. I didn't tell her about this date. I've made a point of not mentioning any male prospect unless they're a real prospect. There's nothing to be gained from getting her excited.

Despite my head start I find myself taking the wrong exit off Ancoats, circling round and encroaching the bus lane on Oldham Street. If I get fined for this and Small tooth-boy and I do get married, I'm sending him an invoice.

My unplanned tour of Manchester town means that we arrive at practically the same time, bumping into each other outside the entrance. This makes things even worse, as our date is no longer within the confines of the café, it's spilled out into the very busy, very visible street.

Neither of us know who should enter first. I'm not sure if I should open the door, or if he's about to. He retreats back and gestures with his hand to lead the way, so I duly oblige.

The café is overcrowded with what looks like other couples, who have escaped the bitter cold for a warm drink. As a result, we have no choice but to sit near the draughty door, on back-less leather stools. I take off my winter coat, though he keeps his khaki-coloured fleece on. Maybe it's part of his overall look.

"God, it's bloody freezing," he announces with an exaggerated shudder as we sit down.

Close up, I realise that he indeed is as small-toothed as his picture suggests. When he laughs, his top lip almost disappears but bizarrely seems to scoop up around his teeth so you can't see them. I try my best to pretend I'm not looking at his mouth, but it's hard.

"Shall we get a drink?"

"Yeah, sure," I respond, though I'm not sure of my next move.

He doesn't ask me what I want, so I can't really put in a request. He gets up to join the queue, and I'm not sure if I'm supposed to go with him. *Is he just going to order something for himself?* This is new dating territory for me. Admittedly, I don't have a wealth of experience in the area but from the anecdotes of others, I'm worldly enough to deduce that this isn't proper etiquette in any culture. Even Shy-boy, despite only socialising with his nephews and nieces, knew better than to expect me to buy my own drink. As Small tooth-boy paces ahead, he turns round, realising that I've not joined him. He looks back at me and uses his hands to gesture that I come along too, like a traffic control guy. I guess it's a group exercise, like we're buddies heading to the bar.

I slowly follow him to the queue, casually chatting as if nothing is amiss. "It's really busy in here."

He huffs. "Yeah, I know. Not the best location, is it?"

Well, *you wanted to meet in the city centre during the Christmas holidays*, I think but don't dare say. I look at the menu scribbled on the big blackboard behind the counter. They've got a festive special – cinnamon hot chocolate. Sounds nice.

"What ya having?" He has his hands in his pockets when he asks me this.

Phew! I breathe a sigh of relief that he's not a massive tight-ass. "I'll just have... a green tea. What will you get?"

"I think I'll have a black coffee, set me up for the day."

It's two o'clock in the afternoon.

"Woah, that's hardcore, I can't even drink milky coffee, let alone black coffee," I laugh.

"Oh, you lightweight! I love strong coffee, can't have anything else."

"Next please!" shouts the barista.

"Can we get one black coffee... and... a... green tea," he says, taking his hands out of his pockets, before swiftly returning them to their safe spot.

"Anything else?" The barista punches the order into the till.

Small tooth-boy says: "Nothing for me." He takes his hand out of his pockets and half-points towards me. "Do you want anything?"

His body language suggests it's an empty gesture. I say no.

The barista looks at us both blankly. "That'll be... £5.19 when you're ready." He doesn't know who's paying the bill, and neither do I.

Small tooth-boy returns his hands to his pockets but doesn't retrieve his wallet.

The awkward-ness intensifies.

In the moment, I do something out of character. As Small tooth-boy still hasn't flashed the cash, I say to him: "I'll get these."

I'm expecting a protest and a bit of a struggle. With Shy-boy, I kind of pretended to offer to pay my way but he wasn't having any of it. He might have been timid but he had enough about him to know that the boy pays the bill on the first date.

Julia told me about an old trick she uses, where she reaches for her purse, very slowly, as the bill arrives. In most cases, her date will stop her in her tracks and insist on paying. She'll ask, insincerely: "Are you sure?" knowing full well that they won't renege their offer. On the very rare occasion a guy hasn't stopped her from getting her purse out, she's suggested going halves and never spoken to that boy again. That was her litmus test.

Small tooth-boy has failed this litmus test miserably. No sooner do I utter those three words, he does a Julia on me, asking: "Are you sure?"

Well of course I'm not bloody sure! I'm being fake! I'm pretending to offer in the hope that you think I'm a classy equitable lady who won't be bought. But in reality, I totally want to be bought. On the first date at least.

I couldn't say this, so I half-laugh, more out of nervous shock than anything. "Yeah, of course."

So there you have it. Worse than going halves, I was paying full board for this kept man. Small tooth-boy will now be referred to as Tight-git.

After bill-gate, it was hard to think about anything else on our date. And it was even harder not to find fault with everything Tight-git said. What seemed like light-hearted banter when we would chat on the phone, was more like serious debating akin to Question Time in person.

"What are your plans for New Year's Eve?" I ask.

Tight-git pulls a face, looking shocked. "Well, it's not really our celebration. As Muslims, I mean. It's just a commercial white thing, so I won't be doing anything. Why, will you be out painting the town red?"

"Err no. Not at all. I don't mean celebrate as in clubbing or drinking into the early hours. But I usually do *something,* as it's a day off the next day. I'll be meeting my friend Julia in the early evening. After that I'll catch the fireworks on the TV with my family."

"Is your friend Julia from work?"

"No, from school. She's one of my oldest friends."

"And what will you girls be doing on New Year's? Going to the pub?" He huffs again and with it I get a waft of strong black coffee. It's a smell I hate. The drink of choice for many an old boss and I'd loathe those one-to-one meetings, where I couldn't move from the bitter smell of beans, without so much as a drop of milk to diffuse the odour.

The door opens again and a biting cold gust of wind bellows through the café, numbing me in the process.

"No, no pub crawl. We'll just go for dinner somewhere," I reply. "Probably our usual Italian."

"Are you a pasta girl? Or pizza?"

Phew, he's lightening the tone.

"Well, I love eating pasta at home," I say. "But when I'm out I always order pizza. What about you?"

"I don't mind pizza from the takeaway but I'm not really a fan of pizza restaurants. If I'm going out, I usually head to

Rusholme for a curry or a kebab. But at home, pasta is rarely on the menu."

"Well, I guess it's my white town upbringing coming through in my food choices! Though I do love my curry." I'm not sure why I'm justifying my love of pizza.

We stumble upon the halal debate, after I tell him I'd tried lobster for the first time recently. This doesn't go down too well.

His hands are now firmly out of his pockets and he becomes animated, using his hands like an orator to argue his point. "But lobster's not halal!"

"It isn't?"

"No, of course it isn't. Pfft! It's not a fish. Would you eat eels? What about snakes? Think about it." He sips his coffee that I bought.

The door opens again, giving me frostbite. We really do have the shittiest seats in the whole café. The stools aren't affording any comfort either. I catch myself slowly hunching over, so attempt to straighten my back. Tight-git, meanwhile, is sitting tall, chest puffed out beneath his cosy fleece, knees wide apart on the tiny stool.

I segue into a conversation about work. It's my chance to ask Tight-git about his career aspirations. Sadly, he doesn't have any.

He returns his hands firmly into his pockets and says with a shrug: "To be honest, I'm quite happy where I am. For me, I want a job that pays the bills. I'm not one of those types who lives to work."

I expect his bills are minimal as he lives at home with his parents. It doesn't sound like he wants to increase his bills – i.

e. get a house of his own – anytime soon either. As I'm more 'one of those types' who likes work and has genuine career aspirations, I pretty much know that this date is a non-starter.

When we progress the conversation to weekend plans, he launches with: "So my brother and sister-in-law are coming up tonight from London but they're in the bad books with mum as they're going on holiday to Istanbul instead of spending half-term with us." He almost spits out the last sentence, assaulting my senses with another stench of coffee.

I'm not sure what to say. "Oh really? Doesn't your mum like them going on holiday?"

"No, it's fine for them to go once in a while but they seem to go every year. I don't know, I think it would just be nice to spend some time up north with us."

It sounds like it's just as much his opinion as his mum's.

"Have you been on many holidays? Or do you want to travel?" I'm all too aware that I'm sounding a bit pretentious, like Fedora hat-boy. But I can't help it. Tight-git is bringing out the twat in me.

He replies with: "Yeah, it would be nice, with the right person. But let's see who that is," he smirks knowingly.

*Ooh, I hope he means me*, said no girl ever.

I walk Tight-git back to the bus stop. Just before he leaves, he has some final words: "It was really nice to meet you. In fact, I was going to ask if you're free next week..."

He's trying to redeem himself. "But I checked the weather on my phone when you went to the bathroom and it's looking like it's gonna be really windy. I don't fancy sitting on the bus in crap weather."

And that, boys and girls, is the final nail in the coffin. The coffin is now six feet under and pushing up daisies.

On the drive home, I get a call from Sophia, who says she wants an update. I wasn't expecting her to ring me, as she seemed fed up during our last conversation. And though I wasn't planning to bore her with my latest non-starter, her call is most welcome.

She's as straight talking as ever and sounds even more high-pitched on loudspeaker. "If he uses wind as an excuse not to see you, he's not worth your time," she says, voicing the understatement of the century. "And *why* is the weather a problem, anyway? He's on the bloody bus! It's not like he's walking for miles to see you."

I can't help but laugh. Sophia is the perfect tonic after a shit date.

"But it's so disheartening. Why can't I meet someone who's just... normal? Do normal Bengali boys even exist?"

"I'm sure they do," Sophia says, not entirely convincingly. "You just have to keep at it. Remember, you only need to meet that guy who's the one for you. And when you find the right person, you'll just know. There'll be none of this bullshit playing phone tag. The right guy will go that extra mile for you, rather than flaking because the weather is bad. It'll all just fall into place. And I should know, it took me two attempts to find Mr Right!"

"Now that's just being greedy!" I joke. "But enough about my crappy life. How are you getting on?"

Sophia takes a deep breath: "Well, I was going to wait until we met... but as I'm not getting any smaller, I better tell you... I'm pregnant! I've been itching to share my news with you face-to-face but I've been feeling so rotten the last few weeks that I've barely left the house."

I can't help but gasp. So that's why she's been avoiding me!

"OMG! Congrats, that's great news!" I almost shout, which makes a woman stood at the pedestrian crossing with a pram think I'm yelling at her to move along.

Despite only meeting Sophia this year, we've grown close enough to share our struggles. My struggle is finding the right partner. Her struggle is – or was – getting pregnant. So I know that this has been a long time coming for her.

We spend the rest of my journey home discussing her news. She reveals that she's not told many of her extended family yet. Some bitchy aunties were judgmental about her choice of second husband, even making cruel Beauty and the Beast jibes. This makes me feel guilty about my initial thoughts when I met Adnan. Sophia also says that some of her unmarried cousins weren't happy for her. She was having two bites of the cherry, when they hadn't even had one.

Listening to her reminds me of the competitive world in which we women operate and how sad it all is. Though deep down, I kind of get it. While I'm truly happy for Sophia and wish her the best, a really small part of me is jealous. Life is moving on, for seemingly everyone but me. I don't want to be pessimistic, but it's so hard to picture myself even getting married, let alone having children. I can't get past the first date. I wonder whether a family of my own is in my future. Or if I'll be a thirty-something brown Bridget Jones still attending pretend charity events.

# 18<sup>th</sup> January, Not going back home

N ew Year, same old problems. I'm still single and now my pessimism has been passed on to mum. Yesterday, she mentioned the 'B' word for the first time. No, not 'bitch'. She's been calling me that in Bengali since I was 11. But only when I was naughty.

B as in 'Bangladesh'.

While she hasn't outright said it, mum seems to think we've exhausted the boy options in the UK. It doesn't help that Mr Choudhury has clearly depleted his resources and isn't taking her calls.

Mum's mightily pissed off as she's still paying him through the nose. "I'd be better spending that money on nest of tables from IKEA."

It's nice to know my worth.

Now she's entertaining the idea of a rishtaa from back home. By this, I don't mean someone who's living in Bangladesh now. We've received the biodata of a boy who has just moved to the UK. He's here on a student visa, works part time in Domino's and would like to settle in Britain permanently. And for that he needs a wife.

And who recommended such a catch? Interfering Auntie Jusna, who's never put forward any rishtaas. After the drama of Iqbal's wedding, which went against her wishes, she's stepped up the search for a spouse for her youngest daughter. I suspect that this boy is one of their cast offs.

With an AWOL Mr Choudhury leading to a man famine, mum is pushing pizza-boy my way.

*Has it really come to this?*

For the record, the Domino's part isn't my main problem. In fact, I love pizza, so a friends and family discount would be most welcome. If he's studying medicine and the pizza job pays his way, more power to him. But being from back home, the likelihood is that he'll end up in the restaurant trade like most men who come over from Bangladesh, including my brother-in-law.

I've seen it happen all too often. A girl gets married to a boy back home who's got a respectable job. He runs his family business, or is a lecturer, or even a lawyer. He comes to the UK, his qualifications don't translate and his poor command of English means he can't get an office job. So he's left with two options. Start from the bottom of the ladder, become fluent in English, retrain and work his way up to the English equivalent of his job in Bangladesh. Or work in a restaurant, with a view to setting up his own eatery one day. Most men choose the latter option. And I don't blame them. At my age, I wouldn't want to be putting myself through yet more education. That's the reason the majority of the UK's Indian restaurants are in fact run by Bangladeshis. They're full of men who came to this country with big hopes and dreams.

Some men do quite well from it. My brother-in-law started out as a waiter in a restaurant, before moving up the ranks. Now he runs two takeaways, which not only keeps my sister in bling-tastic sarees, she also doesn't need to work. However, I've seen the downside. Big sis had to take the lead and support him financially when he first arrived in the UK. He struggled to find a business opportunity in Manchester, so when the chance of a partnership in a restaurant came up in Bristol, they had to relocate and start a new life. As a result, we barely see big sis these days. Mum keeps our third bedroom empty for sleepovers as eight-hour round trips for a day visit would be unreasonable.

While my brother-in-law has a better grasp of English these days, he's still not quite fluent, so sis fills out the school forms, books the travel insurance for the annual Bangladesh trips and works the computer.

That's the other thing. Sis *never* goes on a proper holiday, beyond Bangladesh. That's more down to her hubby, who says that it's not worth catching a plane unless it's to the motherland. Sis says she's quite happy with this. She says she likes her life.

*But I want a different life.*

I've spent my entire existence sticking out like a sore thumb among my peers. For once, I'd like common ground. I want to travel, not just to Bangladesh. I want to see Bali and Bangkok. I want staycations and date nights. I want a husband who can communicate as well with Julia as he would with my mum. Some may call me a self-hating Bengali. Some might say I'm a coconut, a well-used term meaning brown on the outside but white on the inside. But I'm not. I'm just a girl who wants a husband on her wavelength.

Mum doesn't get this and is more concerned that I'm 26 and unmarried. She's also put off because I've had three failed rishtaa meetings and I don't seem to meet anyone of my own accord. Except I have just started to speak to someone. It's a boy who reached out to me on the dating website (yeah, I'm still doing that shit). But as it's such early days, I daren't mention anything for fear of her getting her hopes up. And mine.

With a fruitless manhunt, she is on my case about pizza-boy. It doesn't help that my cow-bag aunty Jusna keeps pestering for a response.

"Look at his picture at least," mum says.

When I first read his biodata, I refused to see his picture. But just to appease mum, when she asked again, I decided to take a peek at his photo. I figured that if he looks like Hrithik Roshan, I *might* just be more open to the idea of a boy from back home. Or at the very least, I'll get to perve on him. If you don't know who Hrithik Roshan is, look him up. You can thank me later.

Mum shows me his photo. He doesn't resemble Hrithik Roshan. There's not a sharp nose or green-brown eye in sight. This boy is less Greek God, more chubby, with a very round face and plumped up cheeks. He's wearing a red and blue cap. On closer inspection, I realise it's a Domino's cap. In fact – bugger me – he's dressed in his pizza-boy uniform.

It's kind of endearing that he thinks his uniform is impressive. But it's not got quite the same panache as a surgeon in scrubs, a banker in a suit, or a pilot in his uniform. I know I sound like a shallow bitch and perhaps I deserve to be single for my judge-y ways but I can't help how I feel. And I'm still not marrying him.

This becomes quite a sore point at home. Mum is convinced that pizza-boy is destined for great things and that I should see beyond his current occupation and the fact that he's from Bangladesh.

She uses her big guns, in the form of my big sister. "Your sister got married in 'desh. She so happy," mum exclaims.

"And middle sis got married here. And she's so happy," I fire back.

"Yes but it not same for everyone. She had more rishtaas. We be looking a whole year but only met three families. In life sometimes you have to make hard choice. You might turn nose at boy because he's from 'desh. But Beet-ish boys turn nose at you."

Ouch.

I didn't see that coming. But maybe I should have. It's always been the elephant in the room. Middle sis is fairer, therefore in Bengali terms, she is deemed more attractive. So while she could take her pick of the boys, I shouldn't be so fussy. I kind of knew this all along and I really didn't expect Hrithik Roshan. But to hear from my own mum that I should settle as pickings are slim, hurts like a bitch. Mum normally has my back. She's my biggest cheerleader in every other aspect of my life. And if nothing else, aren't all mums supposed to believe that their daughters are princesses? Surely there's a reason for the saying 'a face only a mother could love'. Perhaps mum loves my face but she's not sure if many British-Bengali boys will.

And then I cry. And I don't mean Demi Moore's pretty tears in Ghost. I mean full-on, red eyed, open-mouthed bawling. Mum realises that she went too far. She tries to give me a hug whilst remaining firm on her ground.

"Oh stop. Acha enough!" She roughly wipes my cheeks with her hand. "When it bout marriage, it not about the perfect boy but good boy."

I bawl some more, getting even uglier with each wail.

"And why you cry? Have I said bad? How you live with in-laws in UK if you can't even listen to mum speaking truth? That why Bengali boy better for you, no in-laws to stir trouble."

Kicking me when I'm down will not further her cause.

"I just... I just... I wanted more from my life," I sob. "I won't have anything in common with a boy from Bangladesh."

"Neither did your sister first. Now look at her. She got great life."

At this point dad walks in, clearly wondering what the commotion is.

"Eh heh... What's happening? Who made you cry?" Dad goes into protective papa bear mode.

Mum tutts. "Oh she just being silly. You talk with her? We have details of nice boy from Bangladesh but she's too good and fussy. Wants Beet-ish boy with red passport. Hmmmph!"

Mum rarely involves dad in our squabbles, so this shows that she's getting really pissed off with me.

"Let me see boy's biodata."

This is the first time he's asked to see the details of a prospective suitor. Normally mum shoves the photos and bio-data under dad's nose just to show that she's involved him. This is new and I'm not sure where it's leading.

Dad scans the boy's biodata, taking his time to read the details and saying out loud the bits he can't fully pronounce. This is the most attention he's paid to anything other than the Bengali newspaper. He's heavily invested in his role as mediator.

Then dad really comes into his own. "Look, we're not desperate yet. If my daughter no want to marry this boy, her choice. She been to uni-barsity. He work in chicken shop. No match. No good. She can make bet-ta choice."

Dad doesn't say much but when he does, he makes it count. If it wasn't for Bengali formalities, I would give him the biggest hug. Even though mum seems to call the shots, I always used to think of dad as the strict one. Like most brown families, dad is kept out of the loop on lots of things. When we come home late, mum covers for us in fear that he will hit the roof. I wanted to live away for university, so mum rallied my sisters around to argue the case for me. For my pitiful date with Shy-boy, mum again provided an alibi – she said I'm meeting my 'English friend Julia'.

It therefore comes as a shocker that not only is dad supporting me in the fact that I don't want to meet pizza-boy, he also thinks I can take my pick of the totty. This is hilarious given my current track record. But it's nice nonetheless that he thinks that way. Mum might think times are harsh but at least I'm still daddy's little princess. It also doesn't matter that dad thinks Domino's is a chicken shop. That's just a minor detail. Mum expected dad to back her up, so she's caught off guard and agrees to drop it. For now.

Later that evening I get a call from big sis. Here we go. Since dad didn't support her, mum's gone to Plan B. Big sis, with her perfect life, has been enlisted as an ambassador for marriages back home.

However, her call is not what I expected at all. Instead of getting a short promotional monologue on why I should get married back home, big sis is surprisingly against the idea and has told mum to back off.

"The thing is, you've always done things a bit differently," she says. "You went away to university. You have a great career. I just can't picture you getting married to someone from

Bangladesh like I did. When I was getting married, everyone went back home. It was the done thing. But now things are different. Girls have more choices. You can even find boys on the Internet. There are apparently dating websites specifically for Muslims. You should check them out."

If only she knew.

"Uh, yeah. I heard something about these sites. I'll take a look," I say.

Sis goes on: "I see you more with a modern boy who'll want to go out and about, holiday in different countries and have a good office job. In fact, the first fella that came over really seemed to suit you. It's a shame that didn't come to anything."

For God's sake. I've put the ghost of Tall-boy to rest but clearly big sis is still pining.

"But my point is, I don't think you need to go back home."

I'm elated that big sis has got my back. But I have to ask: "So do you regret getting married back home?"

She sighs. "No, not really. I'm happy with my life. I feel like I've married my best friend. And if I didn't meet your brother-in-law, I wouldn't have had my beautiful babies. But... if I was in your shoes, with a good career, money of my own and so many more options to meet someone, I might have made different choices.

She pauses, as if she's about to say something really profound. "The thing is... when you meet the right person, you won't actually care where they're from, or even what they look like. Even though I didn't get to date your brother-in-law, I liked enough about him to know he'd make a good husband. And as soon as we got married, I couldn't imagine being with anyone other than him, so try to keep a bit of an open mind with these rishtaas."

I'm wondering if she's doing a number on me. "So... are you saying I should meet this Domino's boy?"

"Nah, forget that, he works in a chicken shop," sis snaps back.

I'm really not sure why everybody thinks Domino's serves chicken.

Big sis continues: "What I'm saying is, whoever you meet, whether it's through mum, Mr Choudhury, or even someone you find yourself, don't be so quick to judge. Give people a chance. Sometimes the one that's right for you might not be the person you expect."

I see her point. I vaguely remember when big sis first received my brother-in-law's photo. I must have been around eight or nine but one thing that's very clear in my memory is her response. She took one look before saying to mum: "Take that away! I don't want to see it again!"

I don't recall much more. But what I can't forget is those words and the look of disappointment on my sister's face. Disappointment with the spoils of mum's hunting. Disappointment that after a lifetime of being a good girl, this was her reward. I couldn't blame big sis for being so shallow. She was raised on Bollywood movies, where the leading man is always tall and handsome. My brother-in-law's photo presented quite the opposite – a small-framed man wearing a shirt two sizes too big, posing in front of a mehndi tree. But big sis' icy resolve thawed. She agreed to a trip to Bangladesh to meet him (now that's an expensive date), realised that he was the nicest guy and the perfect person for her.

Of course, no conversation with big sis, no matter how deep and meaningful, can end without a dig of sorts. "What I will say is this... you better get your skates on and start looking. Don't just rely on mum. After all, you're not getting any younger. So there's only so long we can fend off these chicken shop boys."

My big sis – supportive and cutting in one fell swoop. But right now, I wouldn't have her any other way.

After a couple of days of not speaking much, mum and I drop our weapons and agree a truce. She's the first to wave her white flag, telling me that she doesn't want me to marry any old Ahmed. She knows that pizza-boy would have been quite a big compromise but there was another reason she was so keen on him, beyond sheer desperation.

It turns out that my cousin Rashda, who once took her pick from the dozens of rishtaas that came her way, is going through a separation. It's all very hush-hush at the moment but according to Auntie Jusna, Rashda's in-laws had a hand in the matter. They were always a looming presence in her life, casting judgment on everything from where she lived (her husband bought a house next-door to his parents), to her decision to work part-time around the children. Sadly for Rashda, as they criticised her every step, her husband didn't fight her corner.

A decade of marriage and three children later, Rashda decided that enough was enough. She packed her things and moved back in with her parents indefinitely. She hoped, perhaps assumed, that it would be a short-term thing and her husband would come and get her and make things work. But he didn't.

It explains why she looked so gaunt at the wedding. And why she took a back seat in the proceedings. I guess Auntie Jusna didn't want people noticing too much, asking too many questions. In a slightly cruel twist of fate, wedding season isn't quite over for Rashda. It's now her younger sister's time to get married. So she's hosting rishtaas once again but not how she should be – as the respectable big sister who's visiting for the day but as the daughter who couldn't make her marriage work. The daughter who is now holed up back in her old room, packed in like a sardine with her children.

And the saddest part? Chances of Rashda remarrying are slim to none. Even her other-worldly beauty won't make up for the fact that she comes with three kids. As Fiona from work found out, few men want to take on someone else's offspring.

I'm shocked by this news. When Rashda was single, rishtaas would trip over themselves to have a two-minute chat with her. When families came to see her, they would come with gifts of gold rings to signify their interest (come to think of it, I never received jewellery from any rishtaas, not that I'm bitter or anything). Scores of mums would make a beeline for her at weddings to deduce her marital status. Given the sheer volume of men she had to choose from, I don't think anybody expected this to be her fate. It was assumed that she'd marry well and live happily ever after. Girls like Rashda shouldn't end up alone.

The news has got Mum worried about me marrying a boy from the UK and having to deal with the in-laws. So far, each boy I've met has lived at home with his parents, so there's a real chance that the guy I marry will be in the same setup.

Mum explains: "You live very modern life. You got good job and you have to travel and stay in hoo-tel by yourself. You go out with friends. You got freedom. And I don't want you to lose it when marriage happen. If you marry someone from 'desh, they come here, live with you. You can hold on to life you like. If you marry in UK, boy family might not like your work. They have more choice in what you do."

"Well, if that's the case, that boy or his family won't be right for me," I argue back.

Mum huffs. She's clearly at her wits' end with me. "I understand. But everyone show best face in beginning. So you dohno how they really feel inside. Do you think Rashda knew her in-laws would give so much trouble before she got married? She learn afterwards, when too late. Also, may be hard finding a Beet-ish boy that will fit in with your life how you want."

"But at least let me try!" I'm tempted to tell mum that I'm looking online and that I have more options than she thinks. But I decide against it for fear of jinxing myself.

"Just give me some time. I'm not desperate. Like dad says, I didn't go through years of study and hard work to settle. Please, just give me a chance to find someone. Don't give up on me yet!"

Mum has tears glistening in her eyes. "I no give up. I never give you up. I just hope you find boy you want."

And I hope so too.

# 23rd January, A new level of compromise

Mum has agreed to pass up on pizza-boy, much to the annoyance of Auntie Jusna who was hoping to brag that she was the one who plucked me from eternal singledom. That's right, even though she's got her hands full with Rashda's separation and a new daughter-in-law, Auntie still finds the time to meddle in everyone else's affairs.

However, I'm sure it won't be long before the details of another boy from back home are shoved through our letterbox. I hate to say it but as blunt and judgemental as she is, big sis makes a bloody good point. I'm 26 and despite my best endeavours, I haven't made any progress on the rishtaa front.

I have been messaging someone online but it's been so sporadic that I've not got anything of note to mention. All I know so far is that he's two years older than me and he lives in London. The latter point isn't ideal. As mum says, it's hard enough getting married to a boy from the UK and having to deal with any potential conflict with the in-laws. To do this when your own family are hundreds of miles away would be much harder.

However, upon big sis' advice, I've not ruled him out as I'm keeping an open mind. Speaking of which, looking back on my failed non-relationships, I don't think there is anyone that didn't get a fair chance. I met Shy-boy despite my reservations about his lack of conversation. Fedora hat-boy was a prick, Small-boy was a short non-starter and Tight-git was...

well... a tight git. None of these boys seemed like the right person for me.

Though in saying that, none of the boys I've met so far have gone beyond a first encounter. So I'm not sure if Shy-boy might have come out of his shell by date number two, or whether Tight-git would have bought me a hot chocolate second time around. This leads me to wonder, just how much should one compromise when it comes to choosing a life partner?

So far I draw the line at:

- Shorties
- Beardies
- Stingies (is that even a word?)
- Wimpies
- Freshies

With the benefit of experience, the things I feel I now have to accept are:

✓ Someone less qualified than me (it's hard to top a degree and masters).

✓ Someone on a lower salary than me (damn me and my professionally progressive ways).

✓ Someone who lives in another city.

Middle sis has inspired the latter point. She lives in Bradford with her husband and kids and they're ten minutes down the road from her in-laws. She tells me that by focussing on boys primarily from Manchester, or even the North West, I'm really narrowing my options.

"Cast your net wide, you'll catch more fish," she says.

So, I'm taking her advice. Looking at my comprehensive list, I congratulate myself on being pretty open-minded. Now I just need to find that guy.

But then... in this sudden mad-dash to get married, I find myself wondering... what if I already found the guy but let him go? Or more accurately, what if I missed my opportunity to find someone?

Thinking back to my university years, there were guys that were certainly interested but due to my parent-fearing nature, I didn't dare pursue anything. But should I have? If I had met someone then, would my life be better now? If I'd made more effort when I was 20, would I be looking for a spouse in such a hurry at 26?

Then my logic kicks in. If I had indeed met someone at uni, I probably wouldn't have enjoyed the career I have now. I would likely have got married soon after graduating (long courtships akin to Prince William and Kate don't sit well with Bengalis). Also, many of my friends' student day romances didn't stand the test of time. Reena was in a relationship for two years but sadly, what seemed like her big love didn't translate into the real world once she'd left the student bubble. Reality kicked in. So, the guy who repeated his first year because he was too high on weed during his exams, suddenly didn't seem like marriage material. Therefore, despite having a dating head start, Reena's in the same boat as me, on the hunt. She's attending padlock and key events and frequenting her local Gujarati community centre in a bid to find Mr Right. Or as she puts it, Mr Oh-you'll-do-I'm-bored-of-this-shit-now.

Yet even with the evidence suggesting it's good that I waited, I wonder if I waited too long. It's so hard to call. If I looked when I was younger, I may have found a partner before I was ready to get married. But now time is of the essence and I'm ready to meet someone, he seems harder to find.

I know there's no sense in looking back as I can't rewrite the past. Harbouring regrets will get me nowhere and certainly won't help my hunt. But I think I just need a minute to feel sorry for myself, before picking myself up again.

# 1ˢᵗ March, Too good to be true?

One of the biggest perils of online dating is that you really don't know if the person you're talking to is telling you the whole truth. I've heard horror stories of married men pretending to be single, players masquerading as nice Muslim boys and, in less extreme cases, people playing up their qualifications or occupations. Essentially, behind the anonymity of a keyboard you can be anyone you want to be.

In the good old-fashioned arranged marriage world, boys come with recommendations and we can trace back their ancestry (well, we'll discover which village in Bangladesh they're from at the very least). This new online hunting ground is a bullshitter's free-for-all.

And I'm scared.

I'm scared because I can't tell the truth from the BS. As I'm the only one in my family to do the online dating thing, I'm scared of getting it wrong. And by wrong I mean marrying someone I met online and it not working out. Surely that's as wrong as things could go, right?

In Bengali culture, if a marriage is going well, it's all fine and dandy. If it goes pear-shaped, the mud-slinging starts.

"*Oh, it's because he's from a different caste,*" said Auntie Jusna when she reflected on Rashda's failed marriage. This strikes me as ridiculous. Given all the other issues they had, mainly stemming from meddling parents, the caste difference seems negligible.

*"It was never going to work out. She's from another village back home and their people are known to be mouthy,"* went the rumour mill for the broken off engagement of a girl from our community. Funny thing is, the girl in question had never even visited her own village but it still mattered.

*"This is why love marriages don't work. You end up choosing with your heart instead of your head,"* is Auntie Fatima's mantra.

I can only imagine the comments after a failed relationship that began online.

*"The Internet! She advertised herself on the Internet! What a slag!"* It's also worth noting that when you're Bengali, it never takes two to tango. It is invariably the woman's fault. She's the slag. The boy was just tempted.

And why am I so scared now? Because after two dates and possibly a billion non-starter online conversations, I'm now speaking to a boy I like. Or at least I think so.

The guy I was messaging sporadically has become less sporadic.

Truth be told, I'd written him off. In fact, I'd written the whole online dating thing off. As a late New Year's Resolution, I decided that I was going to have a breather from boys on the World Wide Web. I even contemplated shutting down my profile. I was sick and tired of the messages that lead to nowhere. The excitement of a ping in my inbox, followed by a swift disappointment when the boy turned out to be ugly, weird, or worse still – he didn't fancy me back.

Of course that doesn't mean that I was calling the hunt off. Far from it, as with each passing year it's harder to find someone, so I can't afford to take 12 months off to discover myself. I figured that I might have better luck attending some pretend charity events, seeing people in the real world. Plus, mum's signed up with another busybody, though I dread to think what's on their spreadsheet.

I was plodding on and getting *very* cynical. I was beginning to wonder if marriage was even in my future. Or at least whether I'd find a boy I really like. I started to resign myself to believing that if I actually do get married, I might have to settle for somebody, *anybody* and make the best of it. But consciously or not, I kept my options open. I kept my profile live but directed all correspondence from that website to my email's spam folder. I didn't want to completely give up hope, I just needed a break from it all. And I figured that sending messages to spam meant that I won't have to sift through a trough of crap. Instead I can dip into the folder once I'm done with my self-imposed online boyhunt ban.

Great plan, right? Except his message infiltrated my inbox.

At work one day, I was pretending to write a case study when I was actually looking for a new job. I'd been at my current company for three years. I was probably as senior as I was going to get. Plus, I hadn't been on the receiving end of a racially awkward question for months, so perhaps my work there was done in more ways than one. I'd applied for a regional PR manager role and was just checking to see if they'd emailed me back when I spotted a message from him, sitting right in my inbox. I figured that I'd messed up my email settings. When I opened the message, it began with the precursory '*should this be in your spam folder?*' question. Yes, it bloody well should, Mr GMail.

But since it had made the effort of turning up in my primary email, it seemed rude not to read on.

His message was apologetic but not overly so: *Hey, sorry it's been a while since I'd last messaged you. I've been mainly offline, as I had to go to America for work for a few weeks...*

Check him out. The most glamorous destination my job has taken me to is Aberdeen. Even then, we flew on the smallest plane ever. It had propellers. I felt every gust of wind during the 45-minute flight. I feared for my life.

He goes on to say: *And I took some annual leave to visit my parents. So I totally understand if you've already met someone. But hope you're well, anyway.*

If only I'd met someone. But more to the point... Visiting his parents? That suggests he doesn't live with them. This makes him a rare species among unmarried Bengali boys.

After an exchange of messages, I learned that while he's been living in London for three years, his parents are just outside Manchester. This is a total plus as it means he has his own space but is from my neck of the woods originally, so will be making regular visits back home. It's a widely held belief that everyone up north is friendlier and more down to earth, so I'm glad that he's not a southern boy. As it's no secret that I've always wanted to live in London, the fact that he's down there already isn't a bad thing.

He works in investment banking (another win) and shares a flat in central London with an old colleague called John. Not only am I impressed with his setup, it's good to know that he lives with a white friend. Why? Because it means he's not a typical Asian boy who only has brown mates.

When I was at university, some Asian guys and girls I met only ever really mingled with their own kind. Partly this was down to circumstance, i.e. they lived in an Asian area and therefore didn't get too much opportunity to mix with people of a different culture. But for many, it seemed that when presented with the chance to converse with someone who's isn't brown, they'd still rather not.

Having been brought up in possibly the whitest town in the North West, this concept is alien to me. Firstly, I wasn't around my 'own kind' to start with. And while it was hard growing up as the only brownie in the village - staying in when everyone was going out drinking, dodging boyfriend talk - I can't imagine not having white friends. My experience has shaped me and, despite my racially exclusive boy hunt, I like to think I'm pretty open-minded in most other aspects of my life. Given what I know so far, this boy is too. The fact that he's living with his white ex-colleague gives me confidence. He's modern-minded and forward-looking enough. Or if nothing else, I've established that he's not a stone-cold racist.

All of this could also suggest that he's something of a coconut and the other extreme of guy I mentioned. The boy that drinks alcohol, parties like there's no tomorrow and has had a string of girlfriends.

But something felt right. I found myself looking forward to receiving his emails. Actually that's an understatement, I've been refreshing my inbox like a mad bitch on a daily basis since he reached out. And so far I haven't been disappointed. He's consistently kept in touch.

We followed the unwritten rules, graduating from messaging on the site, to emails, before talking.

"This whole online thing doesn't come with a rulebook," he joked. "I wish it did."

"Me too. It's totally new territory. If I'm honest, I don't really know anyone who met their partner on a dating website. Well, nobody Bengali, that is." I remember Sophia's success story.

"I wasn't sure whether to even go down this road, to be honest with ya. Then a few of my Pakistani friends started doing the whole online thing coz they were getting fed up of relying solely on their family. It made me think I should be more open minded. After all, there's got to be a first success story, right?"

"I hope so but I'm not so sure sometimes," I reply, rather too honestly. I really shouldn't spill my heart out to a perfect stranger who I may/may not/most likely won't marry.

He pauses. "It's been a tough journey so far?"

Great, I've opened a can of worms. "Yeah... yeah, to be honest it has. I nearly gave up on the online thing before... well... the messages I was receiving were weird and wonderful so I didn't hold out much hope."

"I know what you mean. The hunt is hard."

He calls it hunting too? I thought that was just my thing.

He continues: "But at least you're still trying and getting yourself out there. A few of my girl mates – who are older than me - are always moaning about how tough it is to find someone but they don't do anything about it..."

We talked like this for a while, putting the dating and arranged marriage world to rights. The difference in speaking to this boy compared to anyone else is that it all felt natural.

And I found myself being more open and comfortable than I usually would.

As we were saying our goodbyes, I had to ask: "Out of interest, what was it that made you want to get in touch with me in the first place?"

"I just really liked your profile name. It was so... different. Some girls' usernames were a bit cringe, to be honest with ya. I think one girl even called herself *Prettylady*. I thought beauty was in the eye of the beholder, or something like that. Anyway, the funny thing about your profile was that for a *Wordsmith*, you didn't give much away. So I guess I was intrigued."

The master plan worked.

We started speaking regularly after that. Conversation flowed as Sophia promised me it would with Mr Right. There were no awkward pauses. Neither of us scrambled for a topic to discuss.

We're yet to exchange pictures. He hasn't asked to see my photo, so I haven't requested his. Sophia tells me that's a good sign, as a more shallow guy would want to see a picture of the girl he's talking to before he gets more invested. She says it's best to just meet and see what he looks like in person. And I think she might be right.

On another call, I managed to address an aforementioned concern by simply asking him how religious he is.

He replied in the same way I would. "Well, I fast during Ramadan and I attend Friday prayers. I don't pray all the time though, to be honest with ya. So, I am kind of average in that respect, really. What about you?"

Luckily we were speaking on the phone so I could sound cool and unassuming in my response, despite thinking I'd uncovered a unicorn among men. He's like the male version of me. His family set up is eerily similar to mine, too. This boy's got three brothers, and a teenage sister. He's the second oldest and his older brother also lives far from home with his wife and kids.

We're now texting every day. It's just small stuff about our daily lives but with more frequency than anyone else I've spoken to. With Tight-git, the whole day would pass and I wouldn't hear a peep. But it seems like this guy is making a real effort to get to know me.

It all sounds good, right?

Well here's the problem - it sounds *too* good to be true. Like I say, anyone can be anyone online. I'm wondering if this guy is spinning a web of deceit. He says *to be honest with ya* an awful lot which makes me wonder whether all the other times he's being dishonest. He really ought to rethink his phrasing.

Speaking of speech, despite his claim of being from up north, he doesn't have a particularly notable accent. For all I know, he could well live in London. But instead of renting a new-build apartment and working in the City, he could be flipping burgers by day before retiring to the council flat he shares with his parents, grandparents and seven other relatives at night.

OK, that might be a stretch, but I could also be right on the money. I've hardly got a winning streak when it comes to finding a suitable boy. Whenever I'm remotely excited, my hopes are usually dashed before I've even had a second meeting. The guy is too small, too timid, or just not interested. Whatever it is, I've seen my dream of finding 'the one' come crashing down around me from the get-go.

I don't want to be so cynical. I want to fill that glass right up. And the Bollywood romantic in me is saying that everything looks positive and I may yet design the life I'd like with a man that isn't a compromise. But I'm trying to quieten that voice in my mind, at least for now. At least until I have conducted some due diligence and seen if this boy's life really stacks up. Right now, I'm not sure if I'm smelling bullshit or roses.

However, due diligence is a tricky thing when only one other person knows I'm online. How do I make some enquiries and conduct something of a man-audit?

During our next conversation, I try to deduce more about him in order to carry out some background checks, though I'm trying to be subtle. I call him while sat in my car after I've come home from work.

"You know what? You mentioned your parents live just outside Manchester but I never asked, whereabouts are they?"

Subtle as a brick.

He hesitates. "If it's ok with you, do you mind if I don't say where I'm from for now? Only because I've not told my parents, or anyone else from my hometown that I'm online. And you know it's a small world, so I'd rather keep it on the down-low at the moment. Is that ok?"

Either he really is just like me, to the point that he's also online on the sly, or the smell of roses just got overpowered by a steaming great shit pile.

"Ah ok, I just wanted to know a bit more about you. It's just that with the online thing, it's hard to tell who's being genuine, so I thought I best make sure that you're not a serial killer," I laugh half-heartedly. Again, subtlety is not my strong suit.

"Oh... I see what you mean," he says, like he's only just figured out this totally rational concern. "I get it. It's kind of a new way of doing things and you're right, there are a lot of fake people. If you want, I can give you some of my close friends' details. They know I've got an online profile."

Thoughtful but his friends could also be in on it.

I thank him for his offer but politely decline and we start talking about weekend plans. Thankfully, he has stuff on, or at least he says so: "I'm going to the Globe theatre to watch Romeo and Juliet with my housemate. Have you been?"

How positively cultured he is. I only ever visit London for two reasons – for work or to see family. So I usually don't see much beyond the hotel with work, or the East End if I'm staying with family. Shakespeare's Globe just isn't on the itinerary.

"No, I've never been to the Globe but I'd love to go at some point. It's on my to-do list," I say.

"Well maybe if you come down to London one day I'll take you," he replies.

God, he's smooth.

He asks what I've been dreading since he came over all pretentious with his Globe theatre plans: "So what are you up to this weekend?"

I'm inwardly cringing with my response but choose to be honest. "I'll be going to the cinema to watch the latest John Wick movie."

After almost being outed by Tall-boy on my distinct lack of hobbies, I decided I should make good on my false claim about being a cinema-goer. I'm taking my little sister as a bonding exercise.

"It's not quite as sophisticated as your weekend plans," I laugh.

"Hey, don't knock the cinema. I watch a movie most Friday nights to be honest with ya. *And* I have a Cineworld annual pass. I went last week as my mate wanted to watch a Bollywood film. I only go to the theatre once in a blue moon, if there's something good on."

Woah now! Hold on a second. He watches Bollywood movies? I'm sold.

We talk for about 20 minutes. I notice mum twitching the curtain from inside. She's probably wondering why I haven't come in yet. But once she clocks that I'm on the phone, she moves away from the window. I'm guessing she's figured out I'm talking to a boy and has chosen to turn a blind eye, modern-minded minx that she is. Dad, meanwhile, isn't so discreet. He taps on my car window and gestures that dinner is ready by putting his hand towards his mouth. Mum quickly ushers him away, likely aware that he's thwarting my hunting efforts.

"I better go," I say. "But let me know how your theatre visit goes."

"Will do. But more importantly, tell me what you think of John Wick, as I wanna see it. I loved the first one."

I head indoors to eat but as I open the door, I hear a ping from my phone. It's from him: *My parents are from Droylsden. Happy sleuthing :)*

I'm elated now he's told me where he's from. But where the *hell* is Droylsden?

# 13<sup>th</sup> March, A revelation

So it turns out that Droylsden is a small town outside Manchester. More importantly, his story checks out. Though conducting research on a boy I met on the Internet, when nobody else knows I'm online, wasn't easy. This is where I really appreciate the value of family background audits. I now totally see why mum calls all and sundry when we're expecting a rishtaa visit.

Being Bengali and 26, I don't have the luxury of getting to know a person over years and years. Though times have moved on beyond the two-meeting rishtaa, we still have a relatively small window to meet someone and decide if we want to marry them. We're not allowed to live with boyfriends or fiances. Once we involve the parents, that's kind of it. We better be sure.

It's too big a decision to make alone. I needed someone... anyone... to validate what this guy was telling me. Google Maps told me Droylsden is the next town from Auntie Jusna, though I'd be loath to let her or any of my cousins in on my online dating secret. They'd have a freaking field day.

I don't want mum finding out, either. On one hand, I'm not sure if she'd approve of me looking for a husband on the Internet. It is unchartered territory. On the other hand, she might commend my resourcefulness but get overexcited about this boy. She'll want a progress report *every single day*. In this very early, fragile stage, I'd rather not get her hopes up. Or mine.

Big sis is too old-school and dad is... well... dad. So I confide in middle sis, as she's my safest bet. From the confines of my bedroom, which is unusually sibling free, I call her to spill the beans.

Surprisingly, middle sis approves. "Let's be honest, we haven't come up with anyone good for you. Other people always suggest their rejects and these professional matchmakers only have a ten-row spreadsheet of contacts. So going online really is your best option."

"I thought that the general view is that dating websites were for losers," I say. "Plus I'm scared people can tell you a load of crap about who they are because there's no way of you checking. What if I end up marrying a serial killer, or someone who's already married?"

"Don't be silly," says sis. "You're not gonna marry someone straight away without getting to know them first. Plus, if you think someone's decent, we'll still do the meet-the-family formalities and do our background checks. So, it's not that different to an arranged marriage. You're just doing a bit of initial filtering yourself. At least that way you can stop the ugly ones from coming through the front door."

I never thought about it like that.

"Plus it's also pretty safe. You don't have to publish your photo, so you can shop around anonymously. To be honest, you should have gone online ages ago. If you did, I reckon you'd be married by now."

She's awfully clued up on this.

"How do you know so much about this digital dating thing?"

She pauses, before dropping a massive bombshell. "Keep this to yourself, ok, coz nobody knows but how do you think I met your brother-in-law?"

I nearly drop the phone. "What? But... but I thought you met through our family. He came to our house and everything. You were so shy?"

I can't believe it.

Sis laughs. "As I say, online dating *is* like an arranged marriage. I came across him on a Muslim matrimonial website. We met up a few times. I guess you could call them dates – though the halal version with no funny business. We also spoke loads on the phone and I just knew he was the one. I told mum on the sly so dad wouldn't hear. She did a bit of investigating into his family. Someone always knows someone. Once mum figured out that his family are OK, she called his mum. His family came around the following weekend. That's the bit you'll remember, when I was *shy*, as you say. Everything else was done through the formal family route. So nobody needed to know how we met."

"So was mum in on it all along?"

"No, mum didn't have a clue about the online bit. I don't know if she'd approve as she doesn't really understand it. Nobody's done it before," she confesses. "Plus, very few people were on dating websites back then. I told her we'd met through friends. The great thing about mum is that she's the master of turning a blind eye, gotta love her for that. She didn't ask too many questions. If this guy's someone you're serious about, you can do the same. We'll be able to fake some sort of connection.

At the end of the day, it's who you meet that counts, not how you meet them."

I need a moment to take this all in. Middle sis has always been street-wise compared to big sis but this has surpassed even my expectations. When I said everyone was online but nobody talks about it, I didn't think that included my own family members. I'm shocked, relieved that I'm not the only one online and pretty annoyed that I spent an unnecessary amount of time feeling ashamed of this seemingly open secret.

"Why didn't you tell me any of this before? I've spent months feeling like I was doing something bad!"

"I dunno. I guess I figured you'd already know to go online. Isn't that the done thing now? It's much less taboo nowadays. And as nobody knows I met your brother-in-law online, I want to keep it that way. Anyway, now you know, you can get off your judgemental high horse and give this guy a chance."

For a family who inform each other about every rishtaa visit, we sure are crap at communicating. I wonder how many more secrets there are.

Middle sis redeems herself by hatching a plan. Her hubby has friends in Droylsden and, armed with the information I have provided, he makes some enquiries. It's exactly as sis promised. In the small - yet convoluted - Bengali community, someone knows someone who knows him. While this person doesn't know him directly, she can vouch that he's from a re-spectable family, who keep themselves to themselves and don't get involved in community gossip. Middle sis promises not to tell anyone about any of this.

When she delivers the news to me, I'm relieved. Then she shares one crucial bit of intelligence: "I'm guessing you don't know this as you haven't exchanged pictures yet. But he's bald."

# 18<sup>th</sup> March, A curve-ball

When I would go all Bollywood and dream about my future husband, hair is just something I assumed he'd have. We haven't swapped pictures, so who knows what the rest of this boy will look like. Part of me isn't ready to swap photos. I'm enjoying getting to know him as a person. I don't want to be disappointed or have him be disappointed when he sees me. For the first time, I'm talking to someone and it feels natural, not forced. We just click.

It also appears that our paths have potentially crossed before. During one of our many conversations, I bring up the subject of dating and the rishtaa process. He's made a couple of home visits of his own and chowed down on samosas lovingly prepared by some prospective mother-in-law. He's also had a few dates in London via the website we found each other on. But more interestingly, he tried his luck at the thinly veiled marriage events in Manchester.

"I've not been to any for a while," he says. "The last one I attended was when I came up north last summer, so it's been nearly a year. They're not really my thing, to be honest with ya. The girls were stuck up and the organiser seemed to be a bit of a knob. He kept promoting himself throughout the event. I guess he wanted first dibs on all the girls there, even though he hid his intentions under the banner of charity."

"But doesn't everyone hide their true intentions in this hunting game? I mean... hold on... I think we were at the same event!"

After the penny drops, we compare notes.

I have to share my most important feedback. "I also thought it was crap but the food was good. Every cloud and all that."

He laughs. "Small world. It's a good thing we didn't meet there. I had other things on my mind. Food-based things. I think I ate about three kebabs. You wouldn't have looked twice."

With my buffet-raiding ways, it was no surprise that he didn't make a beeline for me, either. Plus I was too busy checking out the pharmacist, though I'll keep that bit of info to myself. From this conversation, I've established that we're both greedy gits who prioritise food over fundamentals such as finding a life partner. With so much in common, does hair really matter? In all honesty, I don't know. When I made my comprehensive list of what I could and couldn't compromise on, baldness wasn't something I'd even factored in.

I consult Julia. She's just so excited that I'm finally talking to someone I like. And she can't believe I'm on an online dating site. She's always been worried that I'd fall into a marriage of convenience and miss out on the things she takes for granted, such as date nights and holidays. Equally, she thinks it's mad that I've been chatting to him for nearly a month and I don't even know what he looks like.

"But aren't you intrigued? What if you meet in person and he's ugly? You haven't got the best poker face," she says.

She knows me far too well. I used to always give the game away when we played Chase the Ace in school.

"I know but it's kind of nice. We've got to know each other without being superficial. It's the opposite of swapping biodata, where the photo is the first thing you see. But having this bit of info on him has kind of thrown me. I'm now being a shallow cow which is precisely what I didn't want to be!"

Julia's advice is sensible enough: "Why don't you meet him quite soon. Then you'll know if you like him or not. If you don't, then no worries. You'll easily meet someone else. The main thing is you're getting yourself out there. You're on the bloody World Wide Web! I never thought I'd see the day!"

I ponder her point: *You'll easily meet someone else.* But I don't want to meet anyone else.

I speak to Sophia for a second opinion. She thinks the lack of hair is insignificant. "I've always said this - looks fade but a good personality stays. So who cares if he's bald? Most men end up that way, anyway. If that's the only fault you've uncovered so far then I wouldn't write him off."

I sort of agree. "It's just not something I'd thought about. I don't even know what my mum and family will think if my future husband doesn't have any hair."

Sophia huffs. At six months pregnant, I'm sure the last thing she has time for is my procrastination. "Well, it's a good thing he's not marrying your mum then!" She almost shrieks.

The hormones are making her even more forthright. "Hon, when it comes to finding the right person, attraction grows. If they're kind and you click, then before you know it, you'll fancy the pants off them. But don't let this online relationship drag on. Try and meet him quite soon. That way you'll know whether you have the same rapport in person that you do on the phone."

Sophia is right, mostly. I need to meet this boy pronto, just to put my mind at rest that he's not a complete gargoyle. Though I don't fully agree with her point about looks not mattering at all. A bald head might be acceptable, so long as he's not a total troll.

# 23<sup>rd</sup> March, Being bold

Fortune favours the brave, or something like that. In my case, I don't really require a fortune. I'm doing OK work-wise and I've just scored an interview for the regional PR manager role I applied for. However, I need *all* the good luck I can get when it comes to securing a husband.

I've been brave. Very brave. I stuck two fingers up to tradition, etiquette and every other stiff formality there is and asked this guy out. Before I reveal how this bold move played out, I first must mention that I haven't got a nickname for this boy.

If I was to follow my usual childish format, I guess he'd be Bald-boy. It has a great ring to it and I do love a bit of alliteration. But I just can't bring myself to label him. I like him too much. And everything feels different this time. With every other encounter, there was a catch early on, or a niggling doubt. This seems... right. When we talk on the phone, it's like I'm chatting to an old friend. There aren't any games. None of this *he hasn't called me, so I won't call him* bullshit. We both talk to each other whenever we choose, without overthinking whether either of us sounds too keen.

As it stands, we choose to chat every day, as well as exchanging dozens of texts in between. I've grown used to his message after work, checking in on my day. Not to mention sharing lunchtime food plans. Yep, we're fat foodies.

We punctuate our evenings with sporadic updates. He'll send me a snap of what he's cooked for dinner. Impressively, sometimes it's a nasi goreng. Out of a jar but I applaud the effort, nonetheless. In one such candid shot, he actually sent a photo of his recently purchased Audi TT, which he is very proud of. It certainly trumps my Ford Fiesta. In the shot, front and centre is a guy wearing a red jumper and beige chinos, sat leaning on the car bonnet.

It's him!

Despite neither of us asking to exchange photos, he's read my mind and shared his. Either that, or he wants to see my pic but chivalrously made the first move. He's no Hrithik Roshan but he's not bad either. He's well built and possibly muscular under his bright jumper. He looks to be a reasonable height for Bengali standards, too. As my sister forewarned, there's not a hair in sight. But looking at his picture, that doesn't actually bother me as much as I thought it would. He wears his baldness well. There's no dreaded cone-head or neck rolls. While I wouldn't say he's head-turning handsome, he has a nice smile and round, kind eyes. I'm getting Andre Agassi vibes, as weird as that is. He's cute.

Overall, my concerns about him being a troll have been alleviated. I wonder why he sent me his picture, so I bring it up during our chat that evening.

"Oh, thanks for sharing your car pic by the way... and I noticed someone else in there too."

He laughs. "Yeah, well I figured you must be intrigued as to what I look like and I didn't want there to be any major surprises when we do meet."

"Well, it's comforting to know that you don't have two heads. But what do you mean by surprises?" I ask, though I think I know the answer.

"It's just that, a couple of times in the past, I've started talking to a girl and then they've either been put off after seeing my photo or when we've met in person," he confesses. "Apparently a full head of hair is a pre-requisite for many Bengali girls," he adds sheepishly.

*And fair skin or a hijab is a prerequisite for many Bengali boys*, I think but don't say out loud. I'm actually touched and humbled by his admission. Having been on the receiving end of rejection, I know how shit it can feel. And it takes a lot of swallowed pride to admit what people reject you for. He's definitely more confident than me, as I struggle to acknowledge my perceived pitfalls.

"Well, that's their loss. So I guess the polite thing would be to share my picture with you now?"

"No, you don't have to, I'll see you when we meet."

"And when will that be?"

"Soon, I hope. I'll let you know when I'm up north next," he says.

A few days pass by and we chat as normal but no mention of when he's coming to visit. Then one day, he lets me know he's up north in a couple of weeks for a three-day weekend as he's taken the Friday off. Perfect! I'm waiting for him to ask to meet me. But he doesn't.

The next day, we chat again. I quiz him on his itinerary for the visit.

"Oh, I'll just be chilling to be honest with ya. I've got a few friends to catch up with and I think I'll play squash with them on Sunday morning. And apart from spending time with my folks, that's about it," he says.

*Go on, ask me out.*

"What are your plans?"

"Oh, nothing much. I haven't fully decided yet. But generally I think I'll be free," I say, dropping a massive hint.

*Go on, take my hint. Ask me out.*

He still doesn't.

At this point I'm wondering whether he's a bit of a wet lettuce or just being coy. Or is he stringing me along? My mind is doing a number on me. After I put the phone down, I call middle sis.

She practically screams down the phone. "Just bloody ask *him* to meet up!"

"Really?" I'm surprised. Middle sis seems determined to prove she's a trailblazer.

"Yeah, ask him to meet you when he comes to Manchester. Has it occurred to you that he's not asking you because he's being respectful and is worried that it might seem too forward?"

I'd never thought of that.

Sis goes on: "From what I understand, he's a nice lad from a decent family. Hubby's contact said she's never known of any scandals with any of the siblings. So it could be that he's not sure about how to approach things. And truthfully, you'd rather he is that way, than super confident and asking you out straight away. If he's cock-sure with you, odds are he's done this dating thing *a lot.*"

As she's got several years of life (and possibly dating) experience on me, I decide to take her word for it. I call him straight back. With other guys, there was a bit of chess going on - each was second-guessing the other's move. With this boy, it's not like that. He doesn't play games with me. I don't with him.

He picks up my call almost immediately. "Hey, is everything ok?" Clearly he didn't expect me to call back less than an hour after we've just spoken.

Someone's coming upstairs.

Little sis bursts into our room. "Can I use your phone charger?" She sees me on the phone and mouths "oh sorry!"

I hurriedly pass her my charger and she backward steps her way out. Does she know I'm speaking to a boy? She's being awfully subtle. Or is the universe colluding to help me make this most bold move? I wait for footsteps so I know she's gone downstairs. Once the coast is clear, I go for it.

"Yeah, I'm fine. I was just going to say, when you're up... do you... do you want to meet for a coffee?"

Oh my God! I said it! I asked him out! Shit, what if he says no? Can I take it back?

Luckily, I sense a faint sigh of relief. Heck, I can almost hear a smile crack through the phone. "Yeah, that would be really good. I was thinking we should meet," he says.

Ah, so he *was* waiting for me to make the first move.

"Cool, so let me know when's good for you," I say. "Saturday afternoon is better for me but I can be flexible as I know you've got a lot on and you haven't seen your family in a while."

He's surprisingly accommodating: "Saturday afternoon it is. I'll make time. Just tell me where and when and I'll be there."

I decide against my industrial estate Caffè Nero. "There's a nice deli near my work... but it's outside Manchester so I'm not sure if that's too much of a mission for you," I say, remembering that I work in the arse-end of nowhere.

"No, it's fine," he replies. "Given that I'm already travelling over 200 miles to meet you, a couple more kilometres won't make much difference."

If I didn't like him, I'd think he was a cheese ball. I'm not sure if my standards are just really low but the fact that he wants to see me at my convenience and on my terms makes him a keeper.

We say our goodbyes. It's timed perfectly as mum shouts from the stairs for me to come down for dinner. I practically skip downstairs, smug as a bug that I've asked a boy out. Not just any boy but my perfect guy on paper, bald or not.

# 7<sup>th</sup> April, Glass half full

*Today will be a good day. Today will be a good day.*

I chant this mantra over and over again under my breath, as I get ready.

I've been reading up on the power of positive thinking and how the universe helps you if you give out good vibes. It's something I picked up at a business-networking event last week. And it has worked out well for me so far. I've got past the first round of interviews for the regional manager role. Now it's just down to me and one other candidate. I'm liking my chances.

Even though this level of optimism goes against my core glass half empty ways, I'm really getting into this positive stuff. In fact, I'm wondering whether I've been wrong to be so cynical in the past. Maybe I expected too little of others. Maybe I expected too little of myself.

So here I am, getting ready for my date with minimal no-makeup-makeup (that's a thing where you wear makeup so you look good but it doesn't look like you're wearing any. Clever, eh?) and my uniform of jeans and a blouse.

I've opted for a striped chiffon top, as I've put the pink polka-dot blouse into retirement for now. It hasn't brought me much luck. I'm still rocking a winged eye though, as I'm never knowingly unlined.

Unlike the other dates, where I feel like stepping into the unknown, this is familiar but still exciting. I already think, in my gut, that this person will be right for me.

As I head towards the door mum corners me. "Where are you going?"

I lie and say I'm meeting my uni friend Reena. This is only a white lie. Reena has come to Manchester for the weekend from Birmingham, so I am planning to meet her for the first time in ages. But I won't be seeing her until tomorrow.

Mum smiles knowingly. I think she's guessed I'm not meeting Reena, as my no-makeup-makeup is a little too flawless for a date with a friend but is choosing to be complicit in my fibbing.

She then looks serious and says: "I goin' talk with you but it wait for when you home."

I'm intrigued. "No it's fine, you can tell me now." I put my bag down.

Mum does her over-stretched grimace thing. This won't be good. "You might find out from somebody else as it sooo small world... Auntie Fatima call just now. I never expect to see that lady number 'gain, after she ignore for such long time. She say sorry for ignore and sorry for ignore at Iqbal wedding."

"Ok...?" I wonder where this is headed.

"Anyway, she say that boy getting married. The boy come round last summer. Dark face, tall one. Well, he getting married," mum says, avoiding eye contact. "Your Auntie sound pissed off too. I knew she wanted him for niece."

If I was told this a few months back I might have been gutted. After all, despite my best intentions to meet a nice guy, I kept getting disappointed. I thought that maybe Tall-boy was the best of a bad bunch and the one that got away. But I'm not sad. Not in the slightest. I really do feel like I've met someone better.

Mum then looks me in the eyes to see my reaction. I reckon she's expecting tears.

I smile at her. "Good for him. He clearly wasn't the one for me."

She searches my face. "So you no upset? Tell me! I hope you no upset."

"I might have been upset last year," I confess, "but a lot of time has passed. I think I'll find someone better."

Mum relaxes her grimace with a smile and a big exhalation. "Oh, oh! I was so scared to telling you. So, so glad you're ok. Hoo! I breathe now! And you right, you can do so much better."

Having regained her composure, mum looks at me for a long second, with a smile that suggests she's in on some secret. She's totally sussed that I'm seeing a boy and, from my nonchalant attitude about Tall-boy's nuptials, I think she knows this date will be promising. It's like she's got a sixth sense or something.

As I head out of the door, a thought crosses my mind. Was Tall-boy the Asian Daniel Cleaver? Is the guy I'm meeting today the brown Mark Darcy? Am I the British-Bengali Bridget Jones?

Then I realise that's total rubbish. I know who I am and I'm no Bridget. I'm Helena and I'm writing my own story.

# Author's note

Thank you for reading my book. I hope you enjoyed it as much as I enjoyed writing it. If you'd like to see where our heroine heads next in life, you can get the follow-up, *The Secret Diary of a Bengali Bridezilla* below. And let me tell you, if you think navigating the arranged marriage world was hard, planning a bit fat Bangladeshi wedding is a whole other story...

### The Secret Diary of a Bengali Bridezilla

ONE COUPLE. THREE months. 600 guests (most of whom I've never met) and LOTS of opinions.

Welcome to my big fat Bangladeshi wedding.

To do: -

- Find top makeup artist
- Create meaningful favours
- Outdo my cousins impending nuptials
- Have nervous breakdown?

I've found my dream man but will my wedding day be a nightmare?

# You've heard from Helena, now get the other side of the story....

If you're wondering where it went wrong with Tall-boy, how Shy-boy felt after being told 'it's not me, it's you', or why Fedora-hat boy had such an attitude, wonder no more. You can find out in 'The One(s) That Got Away', which is a catch-up with the boys. This e-book is exclusively yours as a reader of *The Secret Diary of an Arranged Marriage*.

If you sign-up to my newsletter, I will send you this for free. Simply head to http://bit.ly/onesthatgotaway and let me know where to send your copy. It's as easy as that.

# Enjoy this book? Want to read more? The power is in your hands...

Thank you again for taking the time to read my book. It makes my heart happy knowing that people are taking pleasure from my words. It motivates me to write more. I want my book to be read as far and wide as possible, and key to making this happening is having great reviews from readers like you.

Reviews are the most powerful tool in my arsenal when it comes to getting attention for my books. I'm not represented by a global publishing house and I don't have a huge marketing team and endless budget.

But I have something better, that money can't buy – a committed and invested readership. And I rely upon this most important asset, to spread the word.

If you've enjoyed this book, I would be grateful if you could spend just a few minutes leaving a review on the website of the store you bought this from. It can be as short or as long as you like.

# About the Author

Halima Khatun is a former journalist (having worked for ITV and the BBC), writer and PR consultant.

Since she was a child, she knew that words would be her thing. With a lifelong passion for writing, Halima wrote her first novel - a coming-of-age children's story - at the age of 12. It was politely turned down by all the major publishing houses. However, proving that writing was indeed her forte, Halima went on to study English and journalism and was one of just four people in the UK to be granted a BBC scholarship during her postgraduate studies.

She has since written for a number of publications including the HuffPost and Yahoo! Style, and has been featured in the Express, Metro and other national publications. Halima also blogs on lifestyle, food and travel and parenthood on halimabobs.com. This is where she also shares updates on her novels.

You can connect with Halima on Facebook here: www.facebook.com/HalimaKhatunAuthor/, or twitter https://twitter.com/halimabobs.

Having spent years in London, Halima has resettled in Manchester with her family.